DIAMOND

If you liked this story then why not look out for other Kelpies. There are dozens of stories to choose from : ghosts, spy stories, animals and the countryside, witches, mysteries and secrets, adventures and many more. Kelpie paperbacks are available from all good bookshops.

For your free Kelpie badge and complete catalogue please send a stamped addressed envelope to:
Margaret Ritchie (K.C.B.),
Canongate Publishing Ltd.,
17 Jeffrey Street, Edinburgh
EH1 1DR.

DIAMOND

Caroline Pitcher

CANONGATE • KELPIES

First published 1987 by Blackie & Son Ltd
First published in Kelpies 1988

© Caroline Pitcher

Cover illustration by Alexa Rutherford

Printed in Great Britain
by Cox & Wyman Ltd, Reading

ISBN 0 86241 185 8

CANONGATE PUBLISHING LTD
17 JEFFREY STREET, EDINBURGH EH1 1DR

Chapter One

'Pearl,' whispered Jenny, 'be careful. You'll fall.'

The white cat crouched on the balcony rail, high up in the city night. Her tail quivered behind her like a battered sail and her ears twitched at the voice. Her yellow eyes blazed briefly at Jenny and then switched back to their searchlight glare around the tower block.

How could the cat balance on that narrow rail? At any moment Jenny thought she might fall and spin away down onto the concrete far below.

The door from the flat crashed open. The white cat flinched at the noise but did not fall.

'What's Pearl doing on that rail? Come down, Pearly cat!' shouted Billy, stumping towards her.

Jenny grabbed her little brother and hissed, 'Shut up, Billy! Pearl is frightened. She doesn't know where the garden is or why she's up in the sky. But cats don't fall off things.' Jenny wished she really believed that. 'Lions and leopards like climbing trees and mountains.'

'Pearl ain't a leopard,' snapped Billy, 'and if she falls she'll go splat on the concrete and die. She's silly. I like this balcony, it's like a spaceship. Come in Starpilot Bill . . . enemy fighters to your rear! Peow! Peow! Aargh!'

Billy fired pretend deathly beams out into the night and each time the cat twitched, her fur spiked out in fear.

'Billy! Inside at once,' ordered Mum, appearing suddenly in the doorway. 'Come in, Jenny. Pearl will be all right in a day or two. We all will.'

Jenny suddenly thought of Billy teetering on the rail with a blanket round his neck playing at Superman, or pretending to be an Olympic diver at Los Angeles. No wonder Mum was worried.

'You keep away from that rail, boy. We're fourteen floors up. It's not like Rendle Road,' warned Mum, marching him inside. 'Do you hear me, Billy?'

'Yes, Mum, yes.' he cried, squirming out of her grasp and running ahead.

In the sitting room, Mum sank into the armchair and reached for a cigarette from the packet on the bare floor.

'I'm exhausted, Jenny! Still, we've got a lot of it straight, and Tom's coming over later to help me lay the carpet. I hope it fits. This room is smaller than the one at Rendle Road, I think. Don't worry—we may not have to live here for long.' She sighed and then smiled brightly.

'You're putting on your cheerful face,' said Jenny.

'Well, at least this flat is easy to clean,' flashed Mum like a television advertisement. 'There are no rotten floorboards, the ceilings are low and the walls straight. They aren't at Rendle Road.'

'It's boring. I like bumpy old walls. And I feel

stuck up here with no street. And no garden. That's why Pearl is so lost.'

'Cats are always like that. I'll butter her paws. She'll lick it off and think it's home. It's not bad here really, Jenny.'

'How come nobody wants to live here, then?'

'Clever madam. Well, it used to be a show estate. The architect won a prize. But people didn't like living here, too high and too big. It got damp. Now they just house people who get a bit stuck. Like us. Now listen, Jenny, we must keep an eye on Billy even though the balcony rail is high. And I can't let him play outside yet, it's too far down.'

'Don't worry, Mum. I'll stick to him like chewing gum to a cinema seat.'

Her mother smiled and her thin face softened. Sometimes she made Jenny think of a hare with big frightened eyes. She had scraped all her hair back from her face and pinned it into a tiny roll with hairpins to keep it out of the way for the move. Jenny liked her mum's hair when it was loose and bouncy. She hated her own hair which was strong and tightly curled. She tried to flatten it down, but it always sprang up again like wire wool. Her mother said it was like the hair of a lady in a Pre-Raphaelite painting, but Jenny thought it looked like a brillo pad.

'Mum, you're smoking too much. Pooh! Look at your yellow fingers.'

'Yes, my love. You're quite right. It's the aggravation of moving.'

'No it's not. You smoke all the time and then tell yourself off. And you don't eat. But you're always feeding other people.'

'You old nag, Jenny Fothergill,' laughed Mum.

Then there was an angry cry of 'Monkey! Monkey!' and a few seconds later the sound of Billy wailing like a siren. Jenny and Mum hurried to his room.

'Monkey's lost!' bawled Billy. 'I can't find him anywhere.' His face was tired and wet, his chestnut hair all tufty. He looked like a baby again as he clung sobbing to Mum.

Monkey was his Number One toy. Once it had been woolly. Now it was threadbare and had only one staring felt eye. The other one had been cut off during a game of surgeons. For most of his walking life, Billy had trailed Monkey along behind him by its long tatty tail. It wore a bright yellow jumper and a striped scarf knitted by Mum. The stuffing had worked its way down from Monkey's elbows, neck and knees long ago so that the head and knees dangled forlornly.

Monkey had belonged to Jenny when she was a little girl, but Billy had loved it dearly from the age of one. He chewed its ears, rescued it at the very last moment from pretend fires with his toy fire engine and swung it round his head mercilessly, shouting, 'Geronimo!'

Often they had space battles. The Monkey always lost and was dropped on the floor, exterminated as Billy sped on to conquer new frontiers alone.

Now that he was five and at school, Billy hid his dear Monkey from his friends. But at night he was back again cuddling Monkey's limp, brown body.

Jenny put on her glasses and searched through

the big box of toys they had packed for the move. No monkey was to be found.

'Don't worry, Billy,' she told him. 'I'll go back to Rendle Road tomorrow. I bet Monkey's there somewhere. I'll find him.'

'He's hiding. He don't want to come and live in this flat,' wept Billy.

'Of course he does. He'll love it. I'll get him for you.'

'Promise?' The sobs were slowing down.

'Promise.' Jenny hoped the Monkey was still in their old house and not at the bottom of a builders' skip.

'Thanks, Jenny,' said Mum. 'We would lose Monkey on the first night here.' She mopped Billy's red, tear-stained face with a tissue. 'Come on, Billy. Let's find a story. *Snow White*?'

'No, she's stupid. Read me *Jack and the Beanstalk* when the giant gets chopped down,' cried Billy, bouncing on his bed.

Jenny wandered back outside onto the balcony. It was quite dark now. The ghostly shape of the cat still hovered on the rail and the saucer of food was still untouched.

I know how you feel, Pearl, thought Jenny.

A new home. A new school on Monday. Jenny felt queasy with nerves. She had been sad to leave Miss Williams and the class at the little school near Rendle Road. The children gave her goodbye cards they had made, and Miss Williams gave her a big kiss. She would have hated that from most people.

Jenny had lived in the house at Rendle Road ever since she could remember, even when her father was still with them. But the council had finally moved the family two miles away across East London while they modernized the house.

Half of the flats seemed empty. They had not seen anybody else in the block yet but they had heard lots of dogs barking.

Looking out, Jenny felt as if they had left the earth behind and might float away into space. The noise of a police siren and shouting drifted up and then faded. The city lay almost without sound.

Out of the ground a short distance away, there grew two similar blocks of flats punched with a few rectangles of light. Jenny remembered models of housing estates they had made at school for environmental studies. They used juice cartons and shoe boxes and cut out lots of little windows with paper curtains. These windows were either smashed or boarded up.

The spaces between the blocks were dark and eerie, with a few dull lights like eyes to mark the paths. She saw a clump of figures by the lights. They vanished. Jenny stared into the patches of black until they threatened to rise up and swallow her.

From inside the flat the doorbell rang, the first time Jenny had heard it. She went in. Mum was talking to a tall man with lots of black hair.

'Oh, there you are, Jenny,' said Mum nervously. 'This is Tom, come to help.'

'Hello, Jenny,' smiled the tall man. He carefully put down a tool box and then took Jenny's hand in his own large, warm one.

Jenny said, 'Hello' quietly, and quickly took her hand back. She had heard Mum talk about Tom, who came into the library where she worked in the mornings. She noticed that her Mum's cheeks were pink and her eyes bright. And she wasn't smoking. Jenny sighed. Now she had to cope with this stranger hanging about as well as the new flat and new school.

She went back to the balcony. The pale moon looked nearer up here, but as she watched, a cloud drifted stealthily over it, veiling the light.

She wasn't going to cry, even though everything was horrible. She didn't cry much, even when Melvyn Mickleton had said that her legs were as skinny as pipe cleaners and her kneecaps like frisbees.

She rubbed her tired eyes and went to bed, leaving Pearl the cat crouched like a white star against the dark.

Chapter Two

As Jenny went out of the flat the next morning, the door opposite creaked slowly open. A wrinkled face, placed between two shoulders like the head of a tortoise, peered at her suspiciously.

'Oh,' said the woman, 'kids. Didn't know there were kids. Can't stand any more noise. Them above have orgies all the time.'

'We don't make a lot of noise, actually,' said Jenny. 'There's only three of us and a cat.'

Behind the woman she heard scrabbling and snarling and an Alsatian dog poked its head through. The woman grabbed its collar.

'You need a dog in these flats. Keep them out.'

'Who?'

'Them. Got a baby?'

'No.'

'Good. No screaming. If anyone comes my dog'll tear their throat out.'

Jenny loved dogs and had always wanted one. So had Billy. He said he wanted a dog big enough to ride on. Jenny stared at the Alsatian's crazy light-coloured eyes and lolling red tongue and suddenly thought of the wolf in *Little Red Riding Hood*.

The woman's face softened a little. 'Don't worry. I won't let him get you. And tell your mum to watch out for them big black beetles. They come through the central heating pipes. Council keep trying to finish them off but they ain't managed it yet.'

The door closed and bolts slid.

In the lift Jenny held her breath as it plummeted downwards. It was smelly and she half expected it not to stop but to crash underground somewhere. Her mother had already warned her not to go in the lift at night. It was scratched with initials and things like SKINS and KILL PAKIS, SCAG and NF. Jenny didn't want to meet whoever had scrawled these things. Maybe they didn't live in the flats but just came to ride up and down in the lift.

It was a twenty minute journey on the bus back to Rendle Road. The bus whizzed along the edge of the Downs. The trees were just squeezing out their leaves for the spring. The mottled branches were clouded in a lime green haze. How pretty they were, thought Jenny. The banks of the Downs were thick with cartons and old paper, shored up by the wind. Jenny looked back and saw behind the gaunt sentinels of the estate, three tall blocks rising like watchtowers against the sky. With a sinking of her stomach she realized she was looking at her home.

In the night Jenny had heard Mum crying, something she often did. At least the cat had ventured in from the balcony this morning, and now cowered behind a cardboard box in the corner of the sitting room, bristling at unseen enemies.

'Once she washes herself, she'll feel at home,' said Mum.

Billy said could he leave off washing until he felt at home. Mum chased him shrieking into the bathroom. He didn't like the loo in the new flat and after flushing it he would tear out as fast as he could in case monsters came up it.

At the other end of the journey, Jenny hurried along the familiar streets to Rendle Road. On the corner she met Mrs Ho, black coat and white trousers flapping, tripping along with the two littlest Hos. They were jumping all the cracks in the pavement.

'Say hello to Lai-Mei for me,' cried Jenny and Mrs Ho smiled and nodded. Jenny thought it was lovely to meet someone she knew. She couldn't imagine that happening on the estate.

Mrs Ho's older children had been at school with Jenny. They spoke to each other in a ripple of sounds that the other children could not mimic perfectly, however hard they tried.

Jenny hurried towards number fifty-seven, their old house. It shouldn't take long to find Monkey.

Then she stopped short. That wasn't her home!

Overnight, number fifty-seven had been boarded up like a huge packing case. The door was sealed by planks of wood and wore a big padlock as if it were the Bank of England. Corrugated iron with its wicked sharp edge rippled around the bay windows. The house looked blinded. Jenny already hated her new home and now her old one was locked away from her.

'Modernize it,' the man from the council, with the strands of hair combed over his bald patch, had said. 'Damp course, central heating, new bathroom.' He hadn't said they would seal it off from the world with hammer and nails. The workmen must have done it the moment the family left.

'What's up, Jenny gel?' A vast shadow fell over her. There stood the monumental shape of Dolly Jones teetering on white shoes with very high thin heels. Her red hair was piled like a plaited loaf on top of her head and secured with shiny combs. Her lips were scarlet. She was enormous but somehow you would never call her fat.

Dolly Jones had lived next door as long as Jenny had been alive. Walter Jones was thin and bent. He scuttled off to work for the gas board each morning, clutching his tupperware box of sandwiches and a thermos full of nourishing soup that Dolly hoped would build him up. Dolly did not scuttle. She sailed along like a galleon. She carried her arrangement of hair as an African woman might balance a large and fragile water pot on her head.

Dolly pushed before her an immaculate pram frilled with lace, bearing the latest small Jones, Dolores, the only girl. 'Fed up with boys, got enough for a five-a-side team,' said Dolly.

'Oh Dolly,' cried Jenny, 'I didn't know they would board up the house like this. The key's no use now.'

'To keep the squatters out, gel, that's why they done it.'

'But Billy's left Monkey in there.'

'Breaking his heart for it, is he? Well, that padlock's asking for it.' Dolly turned towards her

15

own door and hollered, 'Tel! Come here a minute, Tel!'

Terry Jones was the eldest of Dolly's five sons. The five sons spoilt baby Dolores even more than Dolly and Walter did. Terry never seemed to go to school. Dolly always said there were too many jobs for him to do at home and 'roundabout'. He was often sent to help neighbours.

Tel materialized like a genie from a lamp. He was small for fifteen, hunched like Walter, with a jerky starling's walk.

'What, Ma? Hello, Jenny. New gaff all right, is it?'

'No, it's horrible and now I can't get back in fifty-seven to get Billy's monkey.'

'No problem, Jen,' said Tel. He slipped up to the front door, pulled a knife and a piece of bent wire from his pocket and went to work on the padlock. It took only a minute or two to open.

'I'll have to pull them nails out, they've banged up this door real hard,' said Tel, standing back from the door like an artist surveying his work. He nipped back home for some pliers and a hammer and soon had the nails out and the door wide open.

'You're very clever at this, Tel,' said Jenny admiringly. She did hope no one had been watching.

'That's all right, Jen. Let us know when you've finished inside and I'll shut it all up again. See yer later.' And he followed Dolly as she sailed home.

Jenny ran happily inside. Her eyes took a few minutes to accustom themselves to the gloom. The hall floorboards looked dirty and split without

16

the old carpet to cover them up. The house was dark because of its barricaded windows, and seemed strange without furniture and people. It smelled mouldy and cold.

Jenny couldn't see the back garden because all the windows at the back of the house were boarded up too. It was a pretty garden. There was an old apple tree with a silver trunk. There was a swing. There were flowerbeds, too, in which Jenny had grown candytuft and nasturtiums from seeds brought from school, and along the wall were golden sunflowers like visitors from another planet.

Jenny wondered if the house missed the family who had deserted it for a flat in the sky.

She went up the stairs and into Billy's little room. Her footsteps sounded deafeningly loud on the bare boards. The bedroom was unfamiliar without the usual jumble of bedclothes and toys. The Superman patterns on the wallpaper looked dejected as they swooped down towards an empty room. Empty except for something long and tatty trailing out of the wall cupboard. It was Monkey's tail, with the few fronds of wool which were left of the tassel on the end.

Jenny smiled to herself as she snatched up the monkey, who already felt cold and damp. How pleased Billy would be at the return of his beloved toy!

She closed the door of the tiny room and jumped down the four steps onto the first landing. She was anxious to get out of the house now, and into the sunlit street. Then Tel would fix up the front door again as if no one had been there, and she wouldn't get into trouble.

Jenny scampered down the main stairs towards the sunlit escape of the front door.

Then suddenly everything went dark as the doorway was filled with the shape of a black figure. Jenny stopped, terrified, clinging to the bannister rail. A cloud of menace hung in the hall.

Someone was waiting for her. And she had seen him before.

Chapter Three

Jenny's heart banged like a hammer on her ribs as the bent figure shuffled towards her. Yes, she had seen him before. It was down near the market. A crowd of big boys had stepped off the pavement to get out of his way. They hadn't shouted at him; he was a little too strange.

The old man edged up to Jenny. His brown face was so close now that she could see seams of grime in the deep wrinkles. His matted grey beard was like the wool that sheep leave caught on barbed wire fences. Mum would just have pointed towards the bathroom door as she did to Billy when he was all dirty after digging for kangaroos and worms in the garden at Rendle Road. But Mum wasn't here to help. Jenny was quite alone.

Brass band music, a military march, blared out from a little stereo perched on his shoulder. He wore a tweed jacket several sizes too big, and smart grey trousers held up round his waist by a wide *diamanté* belt. Filthy toes peered out of leather sandals like long potatoes. He had a silk scarf the colour of fuchsias tied round his neck in an elaborate bow. Round his head was a large turban of green and gold glittering lurex fastened with an enormous safety pin like the ones that Dolly Jones used to pin her baby's nappies. Long grey hair curled out from under the swathes of sparkling green and gold.

'Well, dear, we've got a lovely home here, haven't we?' he grinned so that Jenny could see two or three yellow stumps which must once have been teeth.

'No! It's *my* house, and we're moving back here very soon!' cried Jenny.

The grin widened. Jenny saw four stumps altogether. 'It would suit me just fine. And I wouldn't turn you out, dear. Ruby! *RUBY*!' he rasped and switched off the brass band music. 'Ruby!' he shouted again and snapped his fingers. They were gnarled and dirty but festooned with gold rings, some with baubles as big as marbles.

In through the front door scuttled the ugliest animal Jenny had ever seen. It was a small dog with a greyish, matted coat rather like the old man's beard. Its nose looked as if it had been punched back into its head like the concertina part of an old box camera. One eye was completely closed up. The other stared unwinkingly at Jenny. Thick tufts of hair curled over each eye socket like comic eyebrows and round its mouth like a moustache and beard.

The dog slobbered slowly and its beard was all wet. The scraggy tail made a complete loop backwards onto the knobbly spine. The tail could wag, and wag it did, furiously, as the little dog turned its one seeing eye lovingly up to its master.

'This house would do us proud, eh Ruby? A

20

fine palace for us!' grinned the old man waving his jewelled hands. Jenny didn't like his grin. Why didn't Dolly or Tel come looking for her?

'You're not a king, so you don't need a palace!' she said.

'How many kings do you know, may I ask, dear?'

'Well . . . I don't, really. But you're dirty and peculiar and so is your dog. My mother would throw you out! Or make you have a bath anyway!'

Jenny was shouting. She was frightened, but she also felt ashamed, because she'd said cruel things. Suppose he got angry and hurt her?

But the old man cackled with laughter. 'You're right! I don't fit in anywhere, do I? I'm in the wrong jigsaw.

> Why was I born with a different face?
> Why was I not born like the rest of my race?

as the poet says. They all hunt us, coppers and social work geezers, people in suits . . .' He spat, narrowly missing Jenny's shoe.

'I'm sorry I was unkind,' said Jenny. But you are weird, she thought.

He cackled with laughter again so that his eyes became all wet like Ruby's eye. He shook out a beautiful lace handkerchief from the pocket of the vast tweed jacket and wiped his eyes. 'You call that unkind, dear? You don't know just how unkind unkind *can* be! Hounded and hunted, that's us, innit Ruby?'

The little dog gazed at him with her fixed eye, drooling with love.

21

'Where do you live at the moment?' asked Jenny, curiosity mingling with fear. She wasn't sure if he was quite real.

'Live? We live everywhere and nowhere, dear. Where do you live? Same place all the time, no doubt. Why don't you live here any more?'

'We live in a horrible flat on the Swallow Estate. My mum cries and the cat is terrified. We've got to go to a new school tomorrow. It's ugly and we don't know anyone any more.' To her shame Jenny felt hot tears in her eyes.

'Dear me. Dear me.' The old man's voice softened. The little dog whined, its head on one side.

'Dear me. You are unhappy. "The eye of childhood is not fearful or bitter." Same poet, dear. So unhappy. And so young. How old are you?'

'Ten. Nearly eleven.'

'You need to see happily. You need to see differently.'

'But I've worn glasses for years.'

The old man cocked his head to one side. 'Yes. You look just like an owl.'

'Well, I suppose it's better to look like an owl than a witch,' snapped Jenny. 'That's what my dad used to call me, 'cos of my hair.' He never said I looked nice, she thought, not once.

'I'll make you see different,' said the old man. 'I'll have a rummage in my magic bag.'

Over his shoulder this man had a big black bag with a huge clasp shaped like a bird made from white pearl and black jet.

'My magpie bag, dear, a treasure hoard. I spend my life looking and finding. I do like a rummage.

Nice magpie, isn't it?' He smacked his lips in anticipation.

'Miss Williams played us a piece of music once called "The Thieving Magpie",' commented Jenny.

The old man glanced at her sharply. 'Thieving is a word I don't like, dear. Seek and ye shall find. Ask and it won't be given.'

Then out of the black magpie bag he took a packet of buttercream biscuits, two bars of chocolate, some silken scarves all the colours of the rainbow, a thick gold chain, a bunch of bananas like fat yellow fingers, a tin opener, a tin of dog food, a packet of tea bags, a small bright blue shiny kettle and a giant box of matches. These he arranged neatly on the staircase, next to his stereo. It looked like a pretend shop.

'Very nice, mister,' said Jenny, puzzled.

'Hang on, dear, that's just my provisions, my bread of life, et cetera.' He ferreted further and Jenny could hear chinkings and rustlings from deep inside his magpie bag.

'Come out, come out, whatever you are!' he cried. 'Aha!' Out came his brown claw-like hand, its long dirty finger nails holding a heavy silver chain. On the chain whirled a big crystal, beaming out colours like the light in a lighthouse. Little seas of crimson, violet and gold danced on the wall as the jewel with its many slanted sides split and spun the bright rays of sunlight from the doorway.

'There!' cackled the old man and his tufted eyebrows flew up and down in excitement. 'This

23

is no rough diamond. Look at all the little sides, so carefully cut. Here. Take it.'

Jenny sighed as she looked at the jewel. 'It's beautiful. Is it very precious?'

'That would be telling. Now take this as a gift from me.' The old man's eyes were deep green as he stared at her. Jenny did not feel she could refuse. And she did want the jewel. Who wouldn't?

'I can't take a present from a stranger,' she stammered.

'Go on. Look after it for me. Now take off your glasses and look through the diamond, dear. Go on. Go on.'

Jenny took off her glasses and placed them carefully on the stairs. Then she peered into the spinning diamond.

It was like a large room with many corners. There were lots of tiny images, not all complete, in bright colours. The tiny pictures were of the head and shoulders of a man in a turban. He looked wise, like a monk or a sultan and there was a faint golden glow around him. He was smiling.

Jenny glanced away from the diamond. There was the strange old man, dirty feet and all, and his turban green as new lime leaves. He was smiling. But she couldn't decide if he looked wicked, or wise.

'Do you like it, dear?'

'Yes, thank you!' breathed Jenny, and looked again. This time she saw a strange little creature like a noble heraldic beast from a shield or coat of arms long ago. It was like a whiskery little lion—with only one eye. Jenny took the diamond away from her eye and slobbery little Ruby barked and wagged her looped tail.

'They say love is blind, girl,' cackled the old man as he bent to pat his dog. 'What's your name?'

'Jenny. Jennifer Fothergill.'

'Sweet joy befall thee, Jenny. Would you like a biscuit?' he said as he packed his bag. 'Custard creams? Marks and Sparks best?'

'No thank you. Won't you tell me where you got this diamond, please?'

'No, dear, I won't. Just take it and be happy.' In her mind's eye Jenny saw her mother, cross, shaking her head in disbelief that Jenny had not only talked to a weird old man but also accepted a present from him.

'Thank you very much,' she heard herself saying. Mum must never find out. 'What's your name, please, mister?'

'Well, I've no name. It's better, really. It's safer. I wander in the wood of no name, like Alice did.' He bent down close to Jenny and whispered, 'Don't tell anyone, dear. Not a soul. Wise man, fool. Not respectable. Mummy wouldn't like it.'

You bet! thought Jenny. She took a step back. He had a funny smell, a mixture of old chips and incense.

'No, I won't tell anyone. I'm sorry if I was rude. And thank you for this wonderful diamond. But where will I find you if I need to give the diamond back or anything?'

'I'm always around somewhere. But a clever little owl like you will manage on her own, Jennifer Fothergill. You'll make happiness out of your muddle. And the jewel will help. I'm always around somewhere.'

Then suddenly, he wasn't. He snatched up his little stereo and flicked on loud marching music. Then he vanished, and his odd dog with him.

Jenny suddenly remembered Monkey, who lay abandoned halfway up the stairs. In her fear she had dropped him. She retrieved her glasses after almost standing on them.

She ran to the front door, looked up the street and down. There was no sign of the shuffling figure, or his animal attendant.

Jenny fastened the chain round her neck and tucked the heavy diamond inside the collar of her blouse. It was cool against her skin.

She felt excited and a little frightened. Better not tell anyone.

Jenny pulled the door of her old home shut and went to find Terry Jones, to ask him to seal it all up again as if no one had been there.

Chapter Four

On the way home she sat right at the front of the bus in a dream. Her hand covered the jewel. The rest of the world rushed by outside the window.

'Yes dear? Come on darlin',' came a voice from far away. It kept saying 'Yes darlin?' and as she surfaced Jenny realized at last that the poor bus conductor was standing next to her waiting patiently for her fare.

'Where you goin,' dear? You in a dream?'

'Oh I'm ever so sorry,' giggled Jenny. 'Yes, I was in a dream.' She paid her fare. The bus roared away down the road and Jenny wished it would never stop.

Finally when it did arrive, she leapt off and skipped across the concrete, weaving her way through the dumped, windowless cars to the estate. There was a driveway down to an underground car park. Mum had forbidden Jenny to go down there. On the concrete next to this was a so-called play area. Nobody had played there for years. The chains which held the swings were all knotted up. The see-saw was chained up and the roundabout tipped over on its side. The red iron rocking horse was completely rusted over. You had to be really desperate to want to play here!

There was also an old mattress with the springs coiling out like intestines and an abandoned television set. A large concrete trough, which had held plants in the days when the estate won prizes for architecture (before people had lived there very long), was now full of cigarette ends, coke cans and dog mess. The flowers had given up hope and shrivelled away long ago.

NO BALL GAMES it said on the wall. What *could* you play? wondered Jenny. You had to laugh, really. She certainly wouldn't be bringing Billy down here to play. It was like a scrapyard. But when she held the diamond and looked through it, the playground became a workshop of old machines in orange and gold with a scarlet warhorse rollicking through the middle.

'That's better,' she said.

Jenny tucked the jewel safely away again and ran up the steps to the block of flats. These steps looked hard and level, as if they would never wear away, no matter how many feet walked over them. The doorstep of the house in Rendle Road dipped down in a smooth valley, worn down over the past hundred years or so by the feet of all the people who had lived and been there. Parents and children, friends and milkmen, postmen and dogs, grannies and grandads, aunts and uncles, cousins, people who wanted you to vote for them, men from the council, bailiffs—and an old man in a bright green turban. All those feet!

Billy shrieked with delight when he saw his dear Monkey. He grabbed it and covered it with kisses.

'Come on and see your new home, Monkey. We can't go out to play here. No garden, no trees for you,' said Billy wistfully to Monkey, who now sat on his shoulder, its long tatty tail hanging down his back. 'Where were you hiding?'

'He was in your cupboard, Billy. He did want to come with us really, but he ate too many bananas and got stuck in the door.'

Billy gave Jenny a withering look. 'I know Monkey don't really eat,' he said sarcastically. 'Come and see the bathroom, Monkey. There isn't a window!'

'Why bother showing him the bathroom, Billy? You're never in there,' teased Jenny. She gave Billy a big kiss, which he wiped away with Monkey's tail, going, 'Ugh!' and pulling a face.

'You're a good girl to get that monkey. Thanks, Jenny,' said Mum. 'Did you remember your key all right? Suppose you must have done.'

'No, the house was all boarded up so the key was no good. Terry Jones opened the door for me.'

'Opened it for you? Broke in, I suppose. Oh dear. I wish you hadn't, Jenny. Someone might have seen you.'

'You could've found yourself in trouble,' said a voice. That Tom was here again.

'Terry Jones could fix a gas meter at the age of eight and everyone sends for him if they get locked out,' explained Mum to Tom. 'He was born with a bit of bent wire in his mouth, not a silver spoon. It's all right so long as he uses his talents for Robin Hood reasons and doesn't get greedy. Jenny, suppose someone did see you breaking in?'

Someone did, thought Jenny. She said, 'Oh, it was all right, Mum. I wasn't there very long and Tel shut everything up after me. If he hadn't picked the lock, you see, Mum, then I couldn't have got Monkey and Billy would've been heartbroken.'

'Well . . .' said Mum.

'Monkey, my mad Monkey!' shouted Billy, laughing and pushing the skinny Monkey into Tom's arms. Billy has taken to this man, thought Jenny. He didn't waste any time. I'll wait a bit, or more than a bit. See what he's like.

'I saw Dolly Jones, Mum,' said Jenny, 'in her red coat. And Mrs Ho.'

'Well, you had a good time, I can see that,' said Mum, staring at her. Jenny blushed. Mum would guess something.

'You *are* in a good mood, aren't you? Look at her eyes shining,' she said to Tom. 'See anyone else, Jen?'

'Er-no,' said Jenny carefully. She wasn't going to tell about the funny man and his dog.

Her hand flew to her throat. She felt the diamond still safely there. Mum seemed to glance at her hand, but said nothing. Jenny was afraid that the diamond might somehow beam out from under her collar. It felt as if it were burning a hole in her skin.

Because it was new school the next day, Mum cooked Jenny's favourite supper—vegetable curry, raspberries and ice cream. (Also it was *her* favourite.)

Pearl, the cat, lay on her back, her nose twitching at the smell of the simmering spices. Her paws

30

opened and closed with pleasure. Every now and then she rolled over in one swift movement. Pearl had been known to steal curries from the kitchen. She preferred them to the pink jelly stuff in her tins of cat food.

Billy kept running up to Mum and pulling faces of disgust, groaning 'Ugh! Yuk!' and holding his nose in case she had forgotten that he didn't like vegetable curry. He had fish fingers with his mound of yellow rice, and mayonnaise on the top.

Tom stayed to supper. Jenny thought he overdid telling Mum how delicious the food was. Everyone *knew* Mum was a good cook. He was a bit grovelly. Mum seemed to like it though. And he bought a huge bottle of sasparilla for Billy and her, and a bottle of garnet-coloured wine for him and Mum.

After supper Billy was sent for his bath. 'And don't give Monkey another swimming lesson,' yelled Mum. 'You know how long he takes to dry.' She and Tom were still drinking their wine. Jenny slipped out onto the balcony. She took out the diamond and looked down at the city. It looked like another world. Jenny felt as if she was standing on the bridge of a spaceship which had just landed. Dreamily she imagined the creatures who might live in the strange city. Creatures round as dinner plates which cartwheeled along, or silver springs which bounced up to the top of the tall buildings. Or it might be a city of birds, wheeling in circles and roosting high in the tall buildings.

As darkness fell the city became deeper blue. The city in the diamond was for night creatures, soft owls and bats on hushed scimitar wings.

Little animals such as hamsters, dormice, and night people wearing circlets of pale lamps around their heads like kings and queens might live there, sleeping in the daytime.

Then something soft smoothed itself against Jenny's ankle. Pearl the cat looked up at her, closing and opening her mouth in a soundless mew. Of course there would be cats in this night city. Grey and smokey blue cats with long soft fur, white cats like snow ghosts and cats sleek as panthers to slink along high ledges. And those fat black cats with white shirt fronts and whiskers, like smug waiters.

Billy would love stories about this strange city. He'd leave for a while his fantasy of Major Bill fighting enemies from his starfighter, with ray guns and lasers and clueless co-pilot Monkey who got blamed for everything. No need for any more Zap! Peeow! sound effects.

'Jenny! Jenny!' came a cry from far away, and Jenny's mind returned to the balcony. There in the doorway stood a small figure in rocket-covered pyjamas with wet spikey hair and an old toy monkey trailing from under his arm. Quickly tucking away the diamond, Jenny went to kiss him. He smelt clean and sweet from his warm bath.

'Geddoff!' he giggled. 'Mum says you got to bath now.'

In they went, Jenny with her head full of dreams.

Lying later in her new bedroom, she forgot about the night city. The dark corners and shapes were new and strange. What on earth was that big heap crouched in the corner? She stared at it for a long time, widening and narrowing her eyes as she tried to make it into something familiar.

Of course. It was only boxes of books with her winter coat thrown on the top.

You silly idiot, Fothergill, muttered Jenny to herself. In spite of the relief of recognizing the heap, she still felt queasy. Her stomach was floppy with nerves. It was the thought of the next day. Monday. New school, unknown people. It was a long time before she slept.

Chapter Five

And she still felt sick when she awoke. Jenny had never before worried about what was going to happen. Things just happened. Today was quite new.

Jenny's mum had already been to see the headmaster the week before to arrange their transfers. Today she had to take Billy down to the Infants' end so Jenny was left alone.

She had to wait outside the headmaster's room. He said he would be out again soon to take her to her class. The second hand of the electric clock on the wall quivered slowly but stubbornly round and round again. Then the minute hand would move on with a shudder and a click. At sixteen minutes past nine Jenny was still waiting there. Why didn't Mr Spinner come out of his room and take her to her class? Should she knock on his door? Had he forgotten all about her? Had he fallen asleep?

Jenny would be the only new girl or boy starting school today because it was the middle of the term. Everyone else would be settled in and know each other, what to do and where to go. Now she was twenty minutes late as well as new.

Two girls of around her own age walked past carrying a pile of green registers. One wore narrow-toed blue shoes with little heels which made a clacking noise the girl seemed to enjoy. The two girls glanced back over their shoulders at Jenny and then met each others' eyes meaningfully. They went into the office marked 'Secretary,' left the registers and then walked back, staring at Jenny all the time. She felt her cheeks burning but tried to force a friendly smile. The two girls went on staring. Their faces did not change. One of them tossed her head and her smartly cut hair with dyed blond streaks lifted and fell. They sauntered back down the corridor and Jenny wasn't sure whether or not she heard laughter.

The door beside her burst open and Mr Spinner sprang out. He was tall and white and thin, in a very smart suit, not like a teacher.

'Ah, Jane. There you are!' he shouted.

'Err . . . Jenny, sir.'

'Oh, all right, then. Jenny. Let's go at once to your class. I did tell Mr Carr on Friday that you'd be joining us.'

Jenny had to run to keep up with Mr Spinner as he strode down the corridor the same way as the two girls had gone. It was a straight corridor, with no plants or pictures. In her other school, every space was filled with something by somebody. There were stick figures and bright blobs of paint from the nursery, and delicate drawings in pen and ink by the fourth years. And there were lots of plants in pots, busy lizzies, geraniums and ivy. Nothing like that here.

Long-legged Mr Spinner sprang up the stairs

three at a time and along another identical straight corridor. They reached an orange door with a little window of shatterproof glass. Here Mr Spinner stopped and pressed his nose to the glass, narrowing his eyes and making an odd grunting noise.

There seemed to be rather a lot of noise coming from behind this orange door. Suddenly Mr Spinner threw the door open and leapt into the room. The shouting and laughing died down but it didn't stop altogether.

'Mr Carr!' rapped Mr Spinner, his little eyes everywhere but on the plump man who must have been Mr Carr. 'Mr Carr! Come here, dear, come here, come here,' he said, waving Jenny impatiently from where she hung back by the door. She edged forward. She hated standing in front of them all, remembering her glasses, brillo pad hair and skinny legs with dinner plate knees.

'Mr Carr. This is . . . er . . . Jennifer Rothmans.'

'King Size or ordinary?' commented a voice from the back. There was giggling.

Then Mr Spinner shouted, 'Right! Carry on!' and rushed out. Carry on they did.

'Well, Jennifer, let's put you here to start with, shall we, until we see which group you belong to,' muttered Mr Carr.

'My name is Jenny Fothergill, not Rothmans, sir,' she whispered, but Mr Carr took no notice. He showed her a table and chair on its own at the front of the class. The other tables had five or six children at each one. In the sea of faces in front of her, Jenny focused briefly on the two heads, close together, of the girls she had seen earlier.

'Here's a book for your writing. Get Jennifer

a pencil, Sue. We've been writing about, "My Weekend".'

It hadn't sounded as if anyone was writing about anything at all.

How could she write about her weekend? Breaking into a house, taking a beautiful jewel from an odd old man who had no name. It would make a good story, but she mustn't tell it because no one in this room would believe it. She decided to write about things this teacher could safely be told, like moving furniture, how old her brother was, what the cat was called, what they had for supper, that sort of easy thing. That must be what he wanted to read.

Jenny wrote quickly. She kept her head down. She could feel eyes staring at her from behind, but she wrote for about an hour. It was pretty boring first year stuff but she was too nervous to think deeply anyway.

As she finished describing last night's supper, a bell rang. Most of the children were out of the door before the bell had stopped. Last, arm in arm, were the two girls. They glanced down at Jenny's page full of writing, and then at each other. One of them curled her top lip in a sneer. The other wrinkled her nose. They minced out through the classroom door, heels clacking.

'Playtime, Jennifer,' sighed Mr Carr, bending to pick up pencils from the floor. 'Man Kit,' he called to a big Chinese boy who was kneeling on a chair finishing a drawing, taking no notice of little Mr Carr. Coming closer, Jenny saw a detailed pencil drawing of some robots building a space craft. It looked as good as the illustrations in books. Jenny wondered what it had to do with the boy's weekend.

'Man Kit!' bellowed Mr Carr and at last the boy glanced up, eyebrows raised in smooth black arches. 'Man Kit, show Jennifer where the playground is.'

The boy sighed, and tucked his pencil which was sharpened to a needle point, behind his ear. 'Come on, then. You new?'

'Yes,' said Jenny, delighted to talk to someone.

'Can you read?' he asked as they went down the corridor.

'Of course I can!' laughed Jenny. 'I could read a bit before I started school. Mum taught me. And then at the end of Infants I could read anything. Well, almost anything.'

'Well good job,' cos you won't learn here.'

Jenny was flabbergasted.

'Never mind,' he continued in a fatherly sort of way. 'Soon we go to secondary school. Magic! I will do computers and art, all day, all day!'

Jenny spent playtime standing by the playground door. At her other school some of the playground had been made into a garden by the teachers and there was a gardening club, which grew flowers and vegetables. Here there was concrete.

After playtime, Mr Carr shouted, 'Quiet, everyone. Quiet. QUIET, WILL YOU!' as the class wandered back. Last in through the door were the two girls, the one with the blond highlights combing her hair dreamily while the other walked backwards holding up a mirror for her.

'Come on, there, Simone and Natina,' said Mr

Carr wearily, but they looked blankly at him and did not hurry.

'Right then, Class One, I'm going to read you an excellent piece of writing by our new girl, Jennifer . . . Jennifer. Wouldn't it be nice if you *all* wrote like this. See how much she's written? And it's all so neat! Now listen. LISTEN! Dean, stop twanging that ruler. Would you rather read it to us yourself, Jennifer?'

Jenny shook her head violently and wished the ground would open and swallow her up. She stared fixedly at the table top. Mr Carr read from her book in a sing-song, sugary voice, and she thought the whole thing sounded stupid and boring. She had described her family. (Nothing about her dad, of course. Mum said he was very busy indeed with his work—and his new family, Jenny supposed—but sometimes, waking up in the night with a sad weight in her stomach, Jenny believed her dad just didn't *want* to see them. He didn't even want to see Billy, who cried and still wet the bed sometimes. So she never mentioned dad to anyone in case they asked difficult questions. Her dad had just stopped existing, and certainly wasn't going to appear in *this* writing.)

The class actually seemed to be listening, except for Dean, who was tapping his table with a pencil, out of time. Everyone was watching Jenny.

Then Mr Carr read, 'My mother cooked me vegetable curry. She is a vegetarian. She can't go into a butcher's shop because she says it is full of dead bodies. She doesn't understand how anyone can eat animals or fish.'

'What a weirdo!' sneered somebody from the back.

'Bet she eats dandelions and stuff like that,' sniggered a blond boy sprawled over a desk.

Nobody listened to the last sentence about the raspberry tart. There was whistling and loud yawning and clucking noises from Dean.

Jenny shouldn't have written that. She should have given nothing away. Mum said most people ate animals and that was up to them. But in England today you didn't need to eat animals, and if she didn't want to, then that was up to her. What was wrong with that? Jenny and Billy could choose what to eat. But the class all thought Mum was a freak for being different. Or some of them thought she was a freak, and the others just followed.

Jenny knew instinctively that she had made trouble for herself.

She kept her head down over the easy maths cards that Mr Carr handed out next. Never again would she write anything secret or personal, in case he read it out.

'You'll have to bring your own sharpener, the school ones go for a walk,' sighed Mr Carr when Jenny showed him her blunt fat pencil after hundreds of sums.

Everyone groaned and looked at Dean.

'It ain't me!' snapped the thin, pale-faced boy. 'It's Norton!'

'Honky Liar!' roared Norton. 'I'll smash yer head in!'

Skinny Dean slipped like a ghost round the back of Mr Carr as Norton lunged towards him. Then he slid out of the classroom door and away down the corridor. Norton stood in the doorway snorting with rage and then lounged sulkily against the wall. He refused to move from there until dinner time, when he got hungry.

'Sue,' sighed Mr Carr, 'go and tell Mr Spinner that Dean has run out of school again.'

Jenny didn't like to look at Norton as he slumped, scowling, against the wall. He scared her. He took no notice at all of the teacher.

Sue came back a few minutes later to say, 'Mr Spinner ain't there and Mrs Argent says he'll be out all day. Meeting.'

At dinner time, Jenny waited to walk downstairs with Man Kit. He was distant, untouched by the row between Norton and Dean. Past Jenny dawdled Simone and Natina.

'Some do have nutters for mothers, or so they tell me,' piped Simone, tossing her blonded hair.

'Veggy whatsit? Seaweed and Paki food if you ask me,' sneered Natina.

After dinner Man Kit went off to play football and so Jenny leant against a wall trying to look as if she wanted to be there. She really wanted to go to the lavatory but there was a hostile-looking group of girls hanging around the doorway. Anyway the toilets smelt, even from where she was standing.

There alone, Jenny daydreamed of a day when her old class had gone to the countryside on a coach. They had eaten most of their picnic lunch by eleven o'clock, except for fatty Ferjana, who was loaded up with a week's supply of jam sandwiches and crisps and kept up a hand-to-mouth

41

action all day. Then they had played in the sun, piling up the sweet hay and jumping on it, and collecting slimy things from the pond.

A tall girl interrupted Jenny's memories. She had long, glossy black hair caught up with pink slides. 'Some people don't eat meat, like your Mum, innit?' she said. 'I don't eat much meat at all. I am Khadiza.' She smiled and skipped off. Jenny felt much happier.

In the weeks that followed she laboriously filled five grey exercise books with maths, three small books with spelling lists copied from the blackboard and three other books with writing. She was bored stiff. Mr Carr responded with hundreds of tiny ticks. The titles for writing would be "My favourite television programme", "What I did yesterday", or "What I would like to do when I grow up". The others wrote about what they had seen the night before on their videos—often it was ghastly things in graveyards. Jenny hadn't got a video, and only one television. 'Fancy not having a personal portable!' sniffed Simone.

Every other day, a young teacher with long mousy hair and hay fever came to hear them read horrible old reading books, with yellow pages and brown stains, full of silly girls, boys and stupid dogs. They had adventures, not that you always noticed.

This teacher said that Jenny was a good reader and could use the school library. It was dark and empty and the books looked as if someone had been trying to eat them. Mum brought her lovely books from the library where she worked in the mornings, and Jenny read those instead.

However, she did find one special thing in the school library. In a huge old blue encyclopaedia there was a long passage all about diamonds. She lugged the book over to the table by the window where it was light enough to read, and hoped no one would come in until she had finished.

Some of the account was too technical for her to understand. But the rest was spellbinding. She read that diamonds are made deep, deep down in the earth, under so much pressure that they sometimes explode when they are dug up. Sometimes they are released by volcanos erupting. And there could be diamonds in meteorites. It sounded like magic to Jenny.

A rough diamond was opaque, and was specially cut into little facets or sides. You had to learn how to do this through years of practice. Suppose you made mistakes! Bit expensive.

Somehow the cut diamond could split light into the colours of the spectrum. That was how her diamond made all these pretty colours in the sunlight. Jenny remembered making colour wheels in Miss Williams' class and spinning them until all the colours merged into white. They had learned about rainbows. It was called refraction.

She read that diamonds were valued in something called carats—not the orange ones—but a way of measuring their weight. The diamond that the old man had given her was huge. How much was it worth? Maybe thousands of pounds, thought Jenny. Her glasses had gone all steamy with the excitement.

There was a horrible bit about men edging their swords and daggers with diamond splinters to make terrible weapons. It took weeks of hammering to break the diamonds into shards like that, and then they put them into the heated, melted sword. A diamond-edged sword meant power and strength.

The encyclopaedia also said that diamonds were supposed to have magic powers. In some religions, they were part of the earth, strong and everlasting, like love which sees change but does not change itself one little bit.

'And what are we reading about, Jane?' boomed a voice. Mr Spinner's long thin shadow fell across her. Panicking, Jenny flipped over the pages of the old volume and whispered, 'Oh, I was just looking through the encyclopaedia—nothing special, sir.'

'Right. Carry on!' screeched Mr Spinner and his long legs unfolded towards the door. He couldn't have seen the page about diamonds, and even if he had, why should he suspect anything?

Back at the flat, the diamond was hidden in an old sock deep inside her wellie in the cupboard in her bedroom. Jenny felt very guilty about not telling her mum. She also had other worries. Suppose the diamond was stolen? Suppose the police found the old man and asked him about it? He knew her name, and where she lived. Did ten-year-old girls go to prison? Tel Jones would know.

Everything was so dreary and awful, except for that jewel. She hated the estate, and school, and so did Billy. Dad was still gone and now a strange man she wasn't sure she liked was hanging around Mum. Only the diamond shone with any brightness. She'd keep it, for a while at least.

Chapter Six

'But where have you been sick, Billy love?' fretted Mum. 'In your bed? On Monkey? Where?'

'Well, you can't see it. But I feel ever so sick. I shall be ever so sick later, at school.'

Mum and Jenny exchanged looks. Every morning now, Billy turned into a woebegone little boy with a whining voice, usually at about half-past eight. It was always worst on Mondays. He'd had pains in the arms, ears, even up the nose and in the fingers. He'd had sick feelings and headaches. His cheeks were as pink and his eyes as clear as ever, and he never felt ill at the weekend. Twice recently Mum had kept him home and taken the morning off work. On both days he had lain in bed moaning and groaning until about ten o'clock and then suddenly bounced out feeling better. 'As if he'd forgotten he was supposed to be ill!' said Mum grimly.

'He doesn't want to go to school, that's why,' said Jenny. She had known right from the start. She would have liked to pretend to be ill herself, but Mum would have seen through it straight away. Billy was only five and for that hour-and-a-half in the morning, he really believed he *was* ill and put on a brilliant performance.

'Oh dear,' said Mum. 'I've tried not to think about him fearing school. It's worse than being ill. But he'll have to go today. I just can't take any more time off work. Oh dear.'

'I'll take him on my own today,' said Jenny. 'You go straight to work, Mum. It might be easier for him if there's only me to say goodbye to.'

Billy's face turned white when he realized that he had to go to school after all.

'They can ring me at the library if you're ill, darling, they've got the number,' said Mum, stroking his hair. Then she hurried off to work looking upset.

Not one word did Billy say on the way to school that morning. His hand in Jenny's was cold and clammy and Jenny felt as if she was dragging him all the way.

When they reached the playground he just said, 'I don't want to go in there.' Jenny wasn't sure why he was upset by his new class. The teacher looked all right even if the room was bare and nothing looked very tempting.

Whenever Mum asked Billy what he had done at school he said sourly, 'We copy numbers. And letters. All day. And make snakes from dirty plasticene. David Martin bit Miss. And he screams and kicks. They don't do what they're told. They don't listen, I can't hear the story. It's too noisy. I don't like it. I like my old teacher.'

If only I could do something, thought Jenny. She said, 'Tell you what, Billy, we'll make a book tonight, like I used to in the Infants at the other school. I'll write a story about you and Monkey going on a magic ship and you can do the pictures with my new felt pens, and maybe Man Kit would do some drawings for us too. Would you like that?'

But there was no reply. 'It won't be long until home time,' she said frantically. Billy looked as if he did not believe in home time. He stumped ashen-faced into the classroom, fighting back his tears. He's got guts, thought Jenny, but why does he have to prove it?

She walked slowly away across the playground and then looked back. His pale little face was at the window, watching her walk away. He didn't wave. Jenny felt like a traitor. She went up to the Juniors' wall and kicked it, hard. She hurt her toe.

Billy had been happy in the reception class at the old school. He used to jump out at Jenny and her mother when they collected him, clutching little heaps of glued rubbish which he said were lorries or rockets. He brought home paintings of beaming faces stuck around with arms, legs and hair, like whizzing Catherine wheels. At home he spent a lot of time telling them the stories he'd heard that day. Especially *Rumpelstiltskin*. He would act it, screaming and writhing on the floor, begging every time, 'Did he *really* split right in half, *really*?' Dean and Norton would make Rumpelstiltskin's temper tantrums seem like nothing, thought Jenny.

That Monday morning, there was a new girl in Jenny's class called Hazara. She didn't know much English yet and looked frightened. There were four Bangladeshi girls in the class now, and Jenny sometimes played skipping with them, but they talked their own language most of the time. Prim Sue was friends with a girl called Christine, and they talked a lot about the horror films they watched on their videos. Jenny hadn't got a video, and she was scared of horror films. Melanie and Samantha played a lot of dancing games, doing all the latest body-popping and breakdance and disco stuff. Jenny couldn't do these. Her long thin legs went out of control and her knees knocked together like bongos when she tried on her own at home. Anyway, the girls never asked her.

Simone and Natina never talked to her directly. They stared at her like a pair of sullen spiders with a silken thread attached to her, waiting for her to do something wrong.

Man Kit and Jenny shared a table with Khadiza and a boy called Faisal. Dean called it Big Heads Table. 'My mum says the teachers give you extra time, Man Twit, just 'cos you're a Chink. And you, Khadiza and Faisal, 'cos you ain't British.'

'Rubbish,' snapped Faisal, 'I was born in Hackney Hospital!'

'Well, my mum says I can't read proper because of all the wogs and Pakis. Anyway, I don't *wanna* read. I gotta video and I gotta portable and a B.M.X. off of my uncle and a lot more things than you lot, and my mum don't read and it don't matter to her.'

Jenny had once seen Dean's mum. She was pale with black shadows under her eyes like Dean. Her grey coat with the hem hanging down made her look even iller. On her legs were thick blue veins like rivers marked on a map. She and Dean lived on their own, and, according to Dean, he did what he liked and never had to go to bed. Dean's mum looked as if the world had rolled over her and left her gasping and flattened. Jenny thought of her own mum with relief.

This Monday, Simone and Natina were flaunting more new clothes.

'We was down the Roman Saturday and they had all smart new stuff,' Simone was telling Sue in a voice sure to be heard by everybody in the class. They seemed to go to a clothes market every Saturday. Simone wore knee-length emerald green sateen knickerbockers and a frilly white blouse. Natina had a bright pink velvet skirt, with lots of zips, and an off-the-shoulder lilac jumper. Both were clacking around in shoes with little heels, and both had mirrored sunglasses perched on their noses. Dean kept snatching off Natina's sunglasses and trying them on, shrieking, 'Look, Norton, look! Cool, man. New York! Look at me, man!'

'Don't act flash,' growled Norton. 'And don't nick 'em!'

'Stupid,' muttered Man Kit, and lowered his arched eyebrows.

Khadiza said, 'A Bangladeshi girl who dress like that with so much money get into trouble. My big brother says girls who dress like that called tarts. Ow. *Ow*!'

Suddenly Khadiza began to cry. She was holding her foot and sobbing. Simone had overheard her and had stamped hard on her foot.

'Cheeky Paki!' sneered Simone. 'Who do you think you are? You ain't got no money to buy

49

smart clothes. You get all yours from jumble sales!'

Jenny leapt up. 'You didn't have to hurt her foot like that, stamping with your stupid shoes. You can't walk on those heels anyway! You're like little girls dressing up in their mothers' clothes. And don't call her Paki!'

'You what?' Simone still wore the strange, mirrored glasses so that she seemed to have no eyes, only black spaces. Jenny could only see a reflection of herself. A block, nothing to look through and nobody to see.

'I suppose you would side with her, your mum being a nutter and eating all that veggy muck. You've got no more clothes than she has. Four Eyes Fothergill with your wild woolly hair! Like an old witch. Bet you got nits in it! Come to this school new and do lots of work and think you're something special! You ain't!'

'I don't think I'm special!' cried Jenny. 'I just wish everyone here didn't hate everyone else, and I wish you weren't so spiteful!'

'Do you really, well, I say, Madam!' Natina joined in with an affected voice. 'Do you really! Friendly with all the Chinks and Pakis, noodles and pappadums!'

'I can be friendly with anyone I like.'

'Can you really? Not with us, in them old clothes. Flea bag! We wouldn't want you for a friend. Four Eyes Fothergill! Flea bag!'

'People don't get fleas. Cats and dogs do.'

'Oh, aren't we just so clever! Nit head! Knock knees!'

Jenny was busting with anger. She sat at her

table with her fists clenched and tears blurring her eyesight. She couldn't write anything all morning.

'Don't worry, Jenny, they're no good, just nasty,' advised Man Kit.

Why couldn't she have kept out of it all like he always did? thought Jenny. But she couldn't stand bullying. If only she hadn't lost her temper.

'Thank you. It don't matter,' said Khadiza.

But it did matter. Why should Khadiza get a red weal on her foot from that spikey heel?

All Mr Carr said was, 'Now then, ladies, calm down. Girls don't fight.'

Stupid man, thought Jenny angrily.

Jenny was determined not to cry. Natina and Simone were whispering to Sue and Melanie and then to Dean and some others. Children kept glancing at her. Natina and Simone kept looking over but she couldn't tell who at because of the sunglasses. Miss Williams wouldn't have let them wear those, she muttered to herself.

'I don't care,' she swore. 'I don't care.' And it was true. Well, some of it. She didn't really care much about not having a video or a television of her own, or lots of clothes. Mum said things like that weren't important, and anyway she hadn't got the money, so tough luck. But she did mind living in that ugly flat with angry people all around, and she did mind Billy being miserable and she did still mind about her dad.

And she minded being called 'flea bag' and 'nit head'. She ought to laugh, but it hurt her. Some of her clothes were old, and second-hand. But they were always clean. Some children's clothes weren't clean. Dean's weren't. And she minded feeling cut off from most of the class and being whispered about.

Right. Jenny decided that she would take her diamond to school the next day. Nobody else had anything like that! She wanted to tell Man Kit and Khadiza about it anyway, if she dare. She was sick of being so miserable. Just having the diamond with her would make her feel special, richer. She imagined Simone and Natina with their mouths falling open in wonder and envy as they looked at that beautiful diamond. That would show them!

Chapter Seven

That evening, Tom tried to cheer Billy up. He promised to take him to the canoe club on the canal if he didn't cry before the weekend.

'Now when I was a little lad,' said Tom, 'I wasn't allowed to speak at all between nine o'clock and four, except to ask to leave the room.'

'Then where did you go, Tom?' asked Billy sleepily. He lay on Tom's knee in his pyjamas, sucking Monkey's paw.

'I went to the loo, of course! That was the only escape. Except to the dinner hall to eat grey mince and frogs' spawn, and pink jelly made in washing-up bowls. If I so much as whispered at school, I got belted. Hard. So you see, Billy, your school isn't really that bad.'

'Tell me more. Tell me about Horace Hoodle.'

'Not again. There was a lad in my class called Horace Hoodle and he couldn't do his sums. And he sucked his shirt. He couldn't even add on one to a number. Teacher would creep up behind him, hissing "One add one, two add one, three add one, Horace Hoodle!" He'd go all shaky and go, "Err . . . three add one . . . err eleven." Teacher belted him round the earhole every time. "Four add one Horace Hoodle—NOW!" "Errr . . . two? Ow!"'

Billy shrieked with laughter collapsing through Tom's knees down onto the floor. Jenny said, 'Poor Horace Hoodle.'

'Who was your teacher, Tom?' asked Billy, heaving himself back onto Tom's knee. 'Was it Mrs Roberts or Miss Williams?'

Tom laughed. 'No, I was at school a long time before they were teachers. My teacher was Sister Mary. She was a nun.

'What's a nun?'

'A woman who works for the church. They wear long dresses and hoods in black and white. Like penguins. And some of them are very strict teachers and terrify little boys and girls.'

'And some of them are kind, generous women who give up their lives to help other people!' cut in Mum. 'Don't you go prejudicing my children with your tales, Tom. And they don't all wear long robes in black and white, anyway.'

Jenny remembered the black and white clasp of the old man's magpie bag. Jet and pearl. Had he got more precious stones in there?

That night she woke up in the middle of a horrible dream. She was glad she'd woken up. Somebody was chasing her but she couldn't tell who because they wore black goggles, like an old gas mask. Billy was with her, holding her hand, but he kept tripping over. They were running down a street of high buildings without doors. There was nowhere to escape. Then with relief she saw a gaily dressed figure come shuffling round the corner. The old man! Her mouth kept opening and shutting and she knew she was calling to him for help, but she wasn't making a sound. She couldn't hear her voice and the old man took no notice.

Then at last he turned round. It was her father. 'Don't be silly,' he said. 'Nobody is chasing you.'

'They are, they are, look!' She pointed to the figures with the black holes where their eyes should be. But her father ignored her. Fear woke her and she lay awake until morning.

Fastening the diamond around her neck that morning, she prayed today would be different.

In the playground before school, Man Kit hurried up to her and handed her a home-made envelope. It was addressed, 'To Billy, from a secret friend,' in beautiful writing. Inside the envelope there were exquisite drawings of dragons, dogs, spaceships and cartoon characters. Man Kit had carefully cut out each figure and made a little tab so that it would stand up. Man Kit told Jenny he would like a little sister or brother, and he'd been upset when Jenny had told him how unhappy Billy was.

'Oh he'll love them, Man Kit! It's like a little theatre. Thank you so much!'

'Too little to cry about school,' pronounced Man Kit, like an old grandfather.

'I feel happy this morning for the first time since I've been at this school,' said Jenny. 'You've made these for Billy, and I've got my diamond with me!'

'Your *what*?' cried Man Kit. Jenny undid the clasp and held the jewel up for him to see. She told him the story, swearing him to secrecy.

'It's so beautiful. I could draw it. You could sell

it, Jenny,' he said, eyes gleaming. 'Then you could buy a computer, and lovely watercolour paints.'

'Who for?' she laughed. 'I'm going to show Khadiza, too. I might show the other children and not tell them how I got it. I could say it's my mum's.'

'They will be jealous,' warned Man Kit. 'You shouldn't show them.'

And Jenny knew that she shouldn't really show off, or make the others jealous. She just felt so hurt. But then Man Kit was a friend. And Khadiza.

At playtime Mr Carr wanted Jenny and Khadiza to stay in and tidy up the classroom for him. 'Mr Spinner is bringing some visitors round, girls. He wants the school tidy. I know I can trust you two ladies to do a good job,' he said.

'I suppose he's gone for his coffee and fag,' grumbled Jenny as the door shut behind him.

'Always girls,' moaned Khadiza, her mouth turned down at the corners. 'Just like home. Always I have to clear up, never my brothers. They cannot tidy, they say. Poor boys! I will soon teach them! Jenny, look at all this scribble.'

All over one of the table tops was scrawled, 'DEAN IS GOOD. NORTON IS NAFF. DEAN IS GRAT AND TRIFFIC.'

'Well, I wonder who wrote that!' sneered Jenny, rubbing away at the scribble with the dirty old cloth from the sink.

Then, 'Ooh, Khadiza!' she whooped as she suddenly remembered the jewel. As there was no one around, she could show her and tell her the whole story. Khadiza thought Jenny should have it made into a proper necklace. She also thought that the

56

old man might be very wicked indeed. 'May be a murderer, Jenny!' she shuddered.

'It's not just that it's beautiful, or maybe worth a lot, Khadiza. I think of stories when I look into it and everything seems better,' Jenny explained. But Khadiza still thought it should be a necklace.

Jenny had one favourite story that she had thought of from the frostiness of the jewel. She remembered it that afternoon at school. It was very hot and stuffy in the classroom. In the cool dream, she was in a land of snow, the sky sprinkled with white stars. Jenny was the ice queen, wrapped in ermine and sitting on a sledge pulled by six reindeer. Silver wolves ran alongside. They skimmed swiftly over the frozen ground to her palace. It shone white against the sky of midnight blue.

The palace had turrets and round windows of crystal. In the garden, dark green trees hung heavy with snow. The garden was full of white creatures, polar bears, doves, swans on a lake, and a glistening unicorn.

The palace had marble steps leading to a huge hall. There were log fires and lots of tiny spiral staircases leading off to the round rooms in the turrets.

There were enough round rooms for all the people she liked best to live in the palace. She'd have Dolly and all the Joneses, Man Kit and his family, Miss Williams, Auntie Rose and her family from up north, maybe Tom, Khadiza . . . maybe Dad. Even the old man would come to see them, with Ruby. If Mum approved. And she imagined Mum and Billy toasting buns over the log fire and smothering them in strawberry jam.

Suddenly the snow lands vanished and Jenny

realized that everyone was barging out through the classroom door. She collected Billy and went home. It was a stiflingly hot afternoon, but in her mind's eye Jenny was rushing through the swirling snow on her sledge, Billy asleep by her side.

The estate was wrapped in a grey shimmer of heat. Some of the tarmac felt soft and sticky underfoot. The rubbish chutes smelt sickly sweet, although there were still three days before they were due to be emptied. Every flat that was occupied seemed to have a stereo turned up full blast, all the windows were opened to the dust and crossed beams of sound throbbed in all directions. People stood on their small balconies, desperate for green gardens.

The old lady with the frantic Alsatian had said that this hot summer would hatch a great plague of beetles' eggs in the flats. Jenny's mum said that was rubbish. There were a lot of bluebottles bumping into things, though.

It was airless in the flat. There was no way of making a cool draught blow right through. Jenny ate her tea and then dozed off to sleep in the big chair.

When she woke, it was still warm but gloomy.

'Into bed, now, love,' said Mum. 'It's that sleepy kind of weather. It's nearly ten. Billy's been alseep since seven and I can hardly keep my eyes open.'

Jenny was still half asleep as she undressed for bed in the small, stitting room. She yawned, but couldn't seem to get enough air into her lungs. Her head ached slightly. Then she had a shock that flung her coldly wide awake.

The chain from around her neck slid to the

58

floor. It must have been undone already and caught in her clothes until she undressed. But no diamond fell to the floor with it.

She searched all over the floor, lying down and reaching her arm right under the bed. She just found some fluff. The diamond had not dropped into the bedclothes either, or rolled under the chair. Time and time again she shook the blankets, turned her boots and shoes upside down and went slowly through each drawer in the chest and through the wardrobe. She did not want to stop and think about the loss.

Jenny knew perfectly well that the diamond was nowhere in her bedroom. She had to go on searching for it, though. What else could she do? She was cold now, as she had dreamed in the ice queen story. But this cold was bleak, hopeless.

When she was too tired to search any more, she collapsed onto the bed. Hot tears streamed down her face and made her lips taste all dry and salty.

'It's gone. I didn't look after it properly. I didn't deserve it. I shouldn't have taken it to school. I wanted to show it off. But I only showed Man Kit and Khadiza . . .' She cried bitterly, burying her face in the pillow so that Mum wouldn't hear her. The pillow became soggy and comfortless with the tears. There was nothing to look forward to without the diamond. Then she had a headache from all the crying so she sat up in bed and tried to think.

The chain had come unfastened and so the diamond had slipped off. But when? And where? It could have fallen off anywhere, on the way back from school, in the playground, classroom, corridor, or onto that hot squidgy tarmac outside the flats. It could have got stuck in there, like one of those Egyptian scarab beetles, imprisoned when the tarmac cooled and hardened during the evening.

It might be lying in the playground like a big raindrop when all the children wandered into school tomorrow. Nobody rushed eagerly into *that* building, so someone would have time to notice it winking up at them. Or they might stand on it and look down to find that it was not a large stone after all. Jenny shivered.

Perhaps the diamond was lying there, in the playground or in a corridor of a classroom. She would go and look for it. Now.

She slipped on her dark jumper and jeans so as not to be noticed in the night. She carried her shoes so Mum would not hear her sneaking out.

It was ten to twelve by Jenny's watch before she heard Mum's quiet footsteps go into the bathroom and then to her bedroom. She heard the door close. She waited a while, hoping Mum would fall asleep quickly.

What if she stepped on a cockroach in her bare feet? She would feel its fat body crack under her toes and scream. She would have to creep past the Alsatian's door, praying he would not hear her and start to bark or scrabble at his door. Then she would have to press the button and wait for the lift to come thundering up. Was there a light on the landing this late at night?

The lift would arrive and there would be that click and a moment of silence before the doors sprang open . . . there might be something dreadful in the lift. Dare she shut herself alone in there?

There were pools of darkness between the blocks of flats, and corners where people or things could hide. And there was the black well of the underground car park. A lot of the lights were smashed in. The streets on the way to school were narrow and would be very dark. Who would be there?

'Too bad,' she said to herself as she tiptoed along towards the front door. It was only a little way, but every step could bring the horror of a fat, crunched body.

Only one more step to the front door. Jenny put her toes down so lightly—and then snatched them back, stifling the scream of disgust which rose in her throat.

When her heart had slowed down, she peered gingerly through the darkness at the floor. Whatever her toes had felt was still there. It had not scuttled away. She peered a little closer. It was the wrong size for a cockroach. It was too large. It had a fat shape, but it was not a fat cockroach shape. And it was a light colour, not black. It was Pearl the cat's toy mouse, stuffing bulging out, chewed tail like a piece of string.

Jenny breathed a sigh of relief. And suddenly she breathed an almost bigger sigh of relief. She realized that the school gates would have been padlocked shut at five o'clock sharp by the schoolkeeper. She would never be able to climb over the walls which had deep frills of vicious barbed wire running along the top. So there was no point sneaking out tonight if she couldn't even get into the school. Just as well. She would have died of fright.

She went straight back to bed. She lay awake and thought.

Now if someone had found the jewel and handed it in to Mr Spinner, he had not mentioned it. He asked about lost property in the hall. He would hold up an anonymous anorak, or wet swimming trunks at arm's length, nose wrinkled in distaste, so that the owner was often too embarrassed to claim them. Last week he had held up a greasy blue comb, dangling from his fingertips as if it were crawling with lice.

'And who . . . *who* . . . does this fine thing belong to?' he sneered. Jenny and most of the class had often seen Dean combing his hair with the blue comb. He was getting more and more scarlet and sweaty with embarrassment as Mr Spinner leered closer at the comb and said, 'In need of a *very* good wash, I'd say! Or a place in the rubbish bin!'

It had to be Simone who gave the game away, turning round and accusing Dean so that the whole school could hear. Poor Dean had to scurry out to the front and have Mr Spinner drop the comb into his hand as if it were a big blue germ.

Mr Spinner might keep her diamond for himself. He might sneak out of school like a suited daddy-long-legs, out to his automatic Volvo, with her diamond in the bottom of his pocket.

Someone else might have stolen it. Dean stole. He was often accused of taking money, pencils, toys, sweets and scissors from the classroom. He made up very complicated tales. Nobody else could follow them. 'Yes, Mr Carr, sir, that's my strawberry rubber what my uncle gave me last week, but Abdul must have found it . . . and then

62

he put it in my anorak by mistake . . . it ain't Sue's dinner money, it's what my mum give me for comics, 'cos she won it, well I buy them on the way home, yea, funny it's the same amount as Sue's dinner money, well . . . leave it out, Norton, you toe-rag! Funny, innit, how I got the same digital as you, Kelvin . . .'

Sometimes he hid things around the room. If whoever had lost things turned nasty, or if they belonged to Norton, Dean would put on a big act of searching and then suddenly shout, 'Oi! Look what I've found! Lucky, wannit?' He had found Simone's gold bangle 'in the bin' just after she had announced that her dad was coming up the school to find the thief.

Dean always seemed to believe his own stories, even when he was caught out. He might be extra crafty if he had something as special as the diamond. Jenny imagined him, skinny shoulders hunched, chattering away to the diamond as if it were alive. She imagined him looking at himself in the mirror, the diamond held against one pale cheek.

Other children at school were more successful in their stealing. Some things vanished and were never found. She might never know who had the diamond. And claiming it might result in some very awkward questions.

No breeze stirred the curtains at her window. They hung limp. The city lay stupefied below, grey and sullen. No lights shone brightly now.

Chapter Eight

'Don't argue, Jenny. Next week I'm coming up to see that Mr Carr and find out what this is all about.'

'No, Mum, please!'

It was Saturday morning. Mum had finished her brown toast and cherry jam, which she loved, because she never had time for breakfast when it was one of her mornings at work. Jenny's toast lay cold and soggy on her plate. She sighed and held it down for Pearl the cat who licked off the Marmite and butter, purring like a motor bike.

'But you've been so miserable, Jenny. I've never known you like this. You're not eating or sleeping properly, and please don't tell me it's the beetles keeping you awake! Something's happened, and you haven't told me.'

'Mum, nothing's happened, honestly!'

Mum screwed the lids tightly onto the jam and Marmite. 'I know you've never settled properly at that school, but these last few days you've been in a dream. You've always lived in your own little world, but never quite like this. I'm going to see that Mr Carr.' She scraped breadcrumbs off the table and dropped them in the bin.

'Unless, of course, you've got something to hide.'

'Please Mum, don't. I don't want you to! I've nothing to hide. I work and work and don't get into trouble. And you always say you can't stand mums who go fussing up to school. Dean's mum is always coming up to complain and *you* said that was half his trouble, Mum. You did, Mum, I remember!'

'Jenny! Look here, if you're still like this next week, I'm taking a morning off work to come up and sort this all out. I can't have you being so miserable. I'm sure it's something to do with school. Although I know you're not very happy here. We've just got to make the best of it. Anyway, I'll find out from that Carr and Weaver . . .'

'Spinner, Mum.'

'Spinner, then. I'll find out what's what. And that will be that!'

Mum slammed the lid on the bread bin and almost threw the plates into the sink.

'Oh,' sighed Jenny, 'I suppose that will be that, then.'

Some part of her longed to tell Mum everything and let her take over, march up to the school and in a mother's magic way find the diamond. Mum would sort it all out.

For a moment Jenny had a fantasy picture of Mum speaking quietly but firmly to Simone and Natina. Their heads would hang, earrings dangling forlornly. Jenny would be standing a little apart, gazing nobly into the distance.

The door burst open. There stood Billy.

'What's yellow and flat and goes round and round?' he asked.

Jenny sighed. 'I don't know, Billy. What *is* yellow and flat and goes round and round?'

'A long-playing omelette!' screamed Billy and ran off.

Mum and Jenny looked at each other and laughed.

'You know it's his birthday soon,' said Mum.

'Yes. I saved some money,' said Jenny and put her toast in the bin.

It was no good. She wasn't little any more, she had to do things for herself. Anyway, Mum wouldn't be able to find the diamond any more than she could. And Mum would think of an adult's reason for *not* finding it, such as it might be stolen, or you shouldn't take gifts from strangers, especially such a strange stranger. And of course she must never sort out other children like Simone and Natina; that would make things far worse.

Mum was distant these days. She spent a lot of time with Tom and seemed to be *his* best friend now, not Jenny's. He was coming round again today. He was all right, and Mum was cheerful with pink cheeks when he was there. With Dad she had often looked tearful and scrunched up. Jenny did feel jealous, though. She told herself it was because everything seemed bad at once.

Losing the diamond was the worst thing at the moment. And somehow she knew that there was only one person who could help. So she had better find him and admit she had lost his diamond.

'Mum,' she said lightly, 'I think I'll go down the high street and have a look in that big toy shop. I want to think what I can get Billy for his birthday. Man Kit said he would do him a big drawing of a space station with lots of little spacemen to cut out. Maybe I'll get him something to do with that.'

'Well don't be late back, love. Tom said he'd take Billy canoeing, and you too if you'd like to go.'

In the toy shop there were some smart lorries and a beautiful soft hippo toy, but they were much too expensive for Jenny. She decided she would buy Billy a sketch pad and a box of pastels in soft shades. They would make a change from the vivid colours of felt-tip pens. And there was some plasticene which claimed not to stick to carpets and things. Mind you, they hadn't tested it on Billy. He could make a mess anywhere, with anything.

Jenny thought, I haven't told Mum a lie. I did go to the toy shop and I'll buy the things next week when I have more money. It's just that I'm going somewhere else as well, to find the old man.

She walked quickly along the busy Saturday pavements. Past the Hollywood Café, losing its second L. There were lots of shoppers inside, drinking plastic cups of grey tea. There was one of those machines with a dirty plastic orange floating on the juice.

Outside the pub next door, men with red faces

slouched on the pavement waiting for opening time. Her old man was not among them.

On she went, past Mr Cool with its green crocodile skin shoes and tiger shirts, past Dallas Bathroom Fittings and Joyleen Ladies' Garments (Wholesale). Past the little shop which baked the best bread in East London, everyone said. She smelt the warm yeasty smell, the freshness of the new bread and felt hungry now. But she hurried on.

The traffic was crawling past. A funeral procession of six shiny black limousines drove very slowly and people stood still to watch. NAN WE LOVE YOU was written in red and white carnations across the first car. The other cars were covered in wreaths. The people in the black cars stared straight ahead and did not speak.

Then Jenny had to pass the green and white tiled shop with its marble slabs continually awash. She had never dared to look closely. The sinks at the back of the slabs were full, she knew, with writhing occupants. Above the shop, it said in fine gold and green lettering, 'E. Wriggler. Importers. Live Eels.' Jenny tore past, terrified that one day she might somehow catch sight of those eels. Well past the shop she opened her eyes properly again.

It was hot. It took about twenty minutes to reach the market. People moved along like snails. The market was the only other place besides Rendle Road that she had seen the old man. A crowd of black and white boys had stepped down off the pavement to let him pass.

It was a special market. All the world went there

on a Saturday. The stalls were either side of a long twisting road.

The very first stall had tiers of summer fruit, glossy cherries, blackberries, strawberries, redcurrants and purple plums. A delicious warm smell hovered over the fruit. There were green water melons like bowls, some sliced through so that they had juicy pink grins with black seeds for teeth.

Suddenly Jenny was flung against a stall. 'Mind yer backs!' roared a little man struggling through under a sack of potatoes. A little way from Jenny's nose a notice advertised 'Mashrums, 30p a quarter'.

'Get yer mashrums here, mum!' screamed the boy behind the stall.

Jenny was pushed and knocked in the tall crowd and had to keep jumping to stop her toes being run over by shopping trolleys trundled along regardless of mere people. 'Wot about yer melons, mum?' screeched a voice.

A frail old man with a black plastic shopping bag eased himself along the front of the stalls by resting himself on his crooked hands. Once he knocked off a pile of apples, but the stallholder just smiled and said, 'Steady, young man.' An old lady with a red woolly hat pulled down over her ears and a thick coat and socks, despite the heat, tottered past with an even older lady clinging to her arm like a bracelet. This older one was so doubled up, that only the crown of her straw hat with its flowers could be seen, not her face. Could she see anything except the ground?

'Hurry up mother,' hissed the one in the red

woolly hat, 'or we'll miss the racing. I want you to win another fifty quid this week.'

There was a stall with veils of net curtaining and one with crochet dolls with big skirts to cover toilet rolls. One stall was piled high with rolls of glistening material in peacock colours. The old man would love it. Where was he? Why wasn't she taller? She was caught in a whirlpool of people.

Then, between bodies, she saw what looked like a shining green turban. Jenny pushed and writhed her way through and someone tutted crossly as she wriggled past. 'Sorry,' she cried to the sullen face.

At last she reached the figure and grabbed the wrist, realizing just too late that this wrist was slender and braceleted and had not got a gnarled old hand on the end. Or a bag with a jet and pearl magpie clasp.

Dark, startled eyes looked down at Jenny. The green sari material was draped around the woman's head, too. That was why she had thought it was a turban. There were no brilliant green eyes. Just soft brown ones.

'I'm sorry, I thought you were somebody else,' mumbled Jenny.

'That's all right, dear,' smiled the woman. Her other hand, the long fingernails painted shell pink, not like the old man's filthy claws, held out green chillies for the stallholder to weigh.

Stupid me, thought Jenny as she turned away, this market is full of people in turbans and African head-dresses and veils. I'd better be careful. Just because I wanted to see him my eye made him up.

It was very hot trapped in this extraordinary

crowd of people. Jenny tried to turn her face away from an especially smelly armpit which was on the same level as her nose. There were scrawny white chickens on the nearest stall, skinny heads dangling. Quickly she looked the other way. There was a crowd of black men, some with dreadlocks, leaning against a record stall. Music was blaring out, with a persistent *woomph chukka woomph*! The base line pulsated through her body and she began to feel dizzy. There was a smell of rotten fruit and sickly incense smouldering in brass holders.

Then she smelt fish. She stared at the blue and silver bodies, with dull eyes and gaping mouths, sprawled over the white slabs. The fishmonger leant over, podgy cheeks and pale eyes rather like fish eyes in his puce face.

'Whadyerwant, gel? I got red snappers, mullet, cod, coley, 'alibut, 'addock, and a nice bit of squid.'

'No, nothing, thank you.' I must ask someone, she thought, someone must have seen him. I feel hot and sick and people keep pushing me. In a minute I'm going to push back, hard. I'd like to go home. It's a long way. Yuk! that fish!

Jenny stumbled against something and looked down to see what it was. It was a large black boot. She looked up and saw above her, like a lighthouse, a policeman's helmet squeezed around a stern white face. Narrow grey eyes frowned down at her.

'Oh, I'm very sorry,' said Jenny, panicking.

'You are in a hurry, aren't you?

'Err . . . yes.'

'Are you lost?'

'N-o. I don't feel very well.'

71

Jenny had never spoken to a policeman before. Behind his dark shoulder she saw another policeman with lots of freckles.

'On your own, hen?' This one had a Scottish accent. What was a Scottish policeman doing in East London?

'Yes. I'm on my own.'

'Looking for someone, are you?' How did he know?

'Who have you lost, hen?'

A pain was stabbing Jenny between the eyes. 'He's old and he wears silky scarves and a green turban.'

'And high-heeled shoes with pink pompoms, no doubt? Real ginger beer,' sniggered the freckled policeman.

'No,' sighed Jenny. How stupid policeman were! 'He wears old sandals.'

'Sounds a right charley to me.'

'Does your mother know about this . . . this friend of yours?'

Jenny didn't answer. The one with the freckles bent down so that she could see his thin moustache in close-up. Some bristles were ginger and some were blond, the same colours as in a ginger cat's coat.

'I think I know who she means. Seen him round here a bit,' said the one with the narrow grey eyes.

'Where? Where?' cried Jenny.

'He don't stay anywhere in particular. Might stay the odd night at Birlington House.'

'Where's that?' she cried.

'Did he ask you to meet him, this wally?'

spluttered the freckled one. He leaned forward again, his face very pink.

'He's not a wally. He doesn't know I'm searching for him. He gave me something, you see.'

PC Freckle straightened up, his pink face sweaty and shining. The two of them looked at each other, raised their eyebrows and then both bent down so that their hot shiny faces loomed into Jenny's blurry vision.

'Did he now! Gave you something, did he? I don't know, making friends with little girls and giving them presents! I think we need to have a nice little chat. I'll call up a WPC for you, my dear.' Steely Eyes reached for his radio and said out of the corner of his mouth to Freckle, 'Sue will get it out of her.'

Their faces seemed to whizz round Jenny like monster animals on a merry-go-round. Noises swelled at her from a distance. 'Get yer tasty taters here mum! Wot about yer laverly leeks!' *Woomph chukka Whoomph chukka Woomph*! Fish and incense. Jenny swayed and felt herself slide slowly backwards and everything went red and black.

She was caught safely and vaguely noticed hairy arms which seemed familiar. She heard Tom say, 'Poor old Jenny. Are you ill, love? Your Mum is ever so worried.'

He picked her up as her legs didn't seem to work any more. They felt like jelly. 'You see, fellas, she said she was just going down the high street, but she's been gone for hours. I think it's the heat made her ill, and she hasn't been eating properly.'

'I see, sir. So you'll be taking your daughter home now?'

'She's not . . .'

'Maybe she's still a bit too young to go out on her own. Some funny people around, you know.'

'Yes, aren't there. I hope she's been no trouble to you, officers. Thank you.'

Before she fainted away completely, Jenny realized how grateful she was that Tom had found her.

★ ★ ★

'Never ever do that again, Jenny, wandering off for hours on your own. Especially when you haven't been well. Thank goodness Tom found you. He had to look all down the high street, the market was a last resort. He was very worried when he saw those police. What on earth did they want?'

'They just asked if I was all right because I tripped over their great big boots.'

'Like PC Plod, were they?'

Jenny laughed. She hoped that half truths did not add up to whole lies. She had told quite a lot since she'd had the diamond.

★ ★ ★

The next morning, Mum said, 'Why don't you come over to the Downs if you're feeling better? You missed out on the canoeing yesterday. There is a festival, with food and steel bands and clowns and things. Billy is like an orang-utan in a cage today so I'll take him over there for a while. It'll be a laugh.'

74

'No, Mum, I still feel a bit weak.' Jenny hoped she looked ill. 'I think I'll stay here, and read or sleep a bit. You go, I'll be all right.'

'Well, lovey, we won't be very long. Half an hour.'

Jenny heard the front door close and shot across the room. She pulled out the A to D telephone directory from the shelf. She ran her finger down the tiny print. Bird, Birdseye, Birdwhistle, Birkbeck, Birks, Birley . . . Yes! There it was. Birlington House. An address in Shoreditch. She dialled the number, trembling with excitement. She didn't know what she was going to say. It was a long time before someone answered.

'Good afternoon. Birlington House,' said a voice. It was a young voice, not the old man's voice at all.

'Oh. Good afternoon. I'd like to speak to the old man, please.'

'Would you really! Well there are about three hundred to choose from. Which one would you like?'

'Oh dear, I'm sorry. Well, I don't know his name. I only met him once. My name is Jennifer. You would remember him even if there are three hundred others. He wears a green turban and jewels and he likes brass band music, waltzes and marches. And he's got a funny dog called Ruby who looks like a goat with a moustache—or a magic beast.'

'Aha. I see,' said the voice, much softer now. 'Yes, Jennifer, of course I know who you mean. He does sometimes visit us. We like to see him. But he doesn't stay here when the Superintendent is on duty because we're not supposed to have dogs here, and he won't abandon Ruby the Fair even for one night. When the Superintendent isn't here, some people turn a blind eye. And so does Ruby!'

Jenny giggled. 'I just wanted to talk to him. Where is he?'

'Who can say? He only comes here in the winter when he really needs the warmth. In the summer he often goes up north. Likes the wild country, he says. Is he in trouble?' The voice was friendly, not like the policeman's.

'I don't think so,' said Jenny, but she didn't feel sure.

'Well you probably won't find him, dear. He's as slippery as an eel.'

He's nothing like as bad as an eel, shuddered Jenny. Black coils and green slime on white marble. Ugh!

'He'll find you if he needs to, the old devil,' continued the voice. 'He's quite something, isn't he?'

'Yes, he is.' The last few hopes Jenny had of finding the old man slipped finally away.

'Goodbye then, Jennifer.'

'Goodbye. Thank you.'

What could she do? Supposing he came back for the diamond and turned nasty because she'd lost it? Supposing the police followed her up?

She lay in the big chair, almost dozing off. Into her mind slipped a picture of the old man in the country, walking across moorland. The night sky was sprinkled with stars and Ruby was snuffling at his heels. He grinned wickedly and did a few dance steps to his band music, holding out his wide trousers like a skirt. Jenny smiled and wished that the old man and his dog were happy wherever they were.

But they were no help to her.

Chapter Nine

In the old encyclopaedia, it said that Amsterdam was the place to buy and sell diamonds. Jenny hoped that there was somewhere a little nearer.

'Mum,' she asked, 'where can you buy real jewels?'

'Real jewels? What are you buying me? A tiara to wear in the library? Pearls for cleaning out the bath?' Mum was beating eggs, sugar and cocoa for a chocolate cake. The mixture slurped and sucked at the sides of the bowl like a chocolate quicksand. Billy was waiting impatiently to lick out the bowl.

'I'm not buying you anything until I'm rich and famous.'

'I wish you'd hurry up, Jenny. There is a jeweller's shop in the high street with lots of gold earrings and platinum and semi-precious stones. But if you're talking about the big time, then it's Hatton Garden.'

'Hatton Garden . . .' It sounded beautiful. Jenny dreamed of a formal garden with lots of little box hedges and trees in tubs, trimmed into spheres and hung all over with big diamonds like raindrops.

'Where is it, Mum?'

'What?'

'Hatton Garden?'

'Oh, it's near Leather Lane Market. Hatton Garden is where all the big jewellers do their wheeling and dealing. Pass me the cream out of the fridge. Dolly will be here in a minute.'

'If she can fit in the lift!' cackled Billy.

'Now then! Anyway it has a ten person capacity.'

Mum loved to feed people. Today, a Saturday, she had made a cake encrusted with glossy *glacé* cherries and hedgehogged with toasted almonds. And there was a dark chocolate cake on the way, which would be sandwiched together with whipped cream and covered in shiny icing. 'Then I'll grate chocolate on the top,' she told Jenny. She loved to spoil people.

When the cakes were finished they all had to be covered. The old lady's warning about beetles had been true. They lived in the central heating system, large and black, hundreds of them. At first, the family had been puzzled by the behaviour of Pearl the cat. She was fascinated by the opening of the heating duct in the sitting room and crouched staring down it as if mesmerized. Was it mice, they wondered?

Then late one night, Mum had gone into the sitting room and switched on the light to find that she had floodlit a pitch with a team of one white cat versus scores of scurrying cockroaches. Pearl was not distracted from her game by the light, but the beetles vanished as fast as their many legs would carry them. Mum screamed and ran as she saw Pearl scrunching up the six-legged intruders as if they were pieces of best smoked salmon.

Jenny was revolted by this story. And now she was terrified of stepping on a cockroach at night in her bare feet. How *could* Pearl eat beetles so fat and squidgy? She had plenty of cat food and tasty titbits.

Billy loved the whole business and gleefully searched for stick legs which he said Pearl spat out and did not eat.

Tom said that in New York there were millions of cockroaches and that the people caught them in sticky boxes called cockroach motels. Jenny covered up her ears and ran out of the room.

Suddenly there was a loud knocking, and there stood Dolly Jones in and around the doorway, a mountain of familiarity in a turquoise silky dress. No coat. It must be a hot summer.

'Phew! Sweating rivers, I am, Carol! You couldn't swing a cat in that lift. Why did they have to stick you all the way up here?' She sailed across the room. 'I don't like that balcony, gel, even if you can see Hackney marshes. Not safe and too small.'

'I know, Dolly, especially with Billy who's not too sensible yet. It's only temporary, till they've done up the house in Rendle Road. I hope so, anyway.'

'This is what they call on telly a dump estate, Carol, to be honest. They don't put families up here permanent. They try to get students and people on their own. I don't see why they should like it either. There's a lot of flats boarded up. We didn't see a soul on the way up, did we, Tel?'

Behind Dolly hovered Tel, hopping from foot to foot and grinning. He parked the candy-striped baby buggy near the door. The buggy bore Dolores, second queen of the Jones household. She sat there regally in a *broderie Anglaise* dress and white socks with pink ribbons, solemnly licking an ice-cream.

Dolly launched herself onto the settee. It dipped floorwards. 'Well, I hope you're not here too long, Carol. Council did start work on your house one day last week but they went for breakfast and never came back.'

'Don't look no different,' mumbled Tel through chocolate cake. Tel had a huge appetite but stayed thin and pointy like a shadow puppet. Jenny offered him some fruit loaf. He accepted through chocolate-rimmed lips. Billy stared, enchanted by the speed at which Tel ate.

'Don't let us interrupt you, Tel boy,' chortled Dolly. 'Of course, he's starved indoors, you know.' Dolly shook with laughter from her face right down to her treacherous gold sandals. 'It's your delicious cakes, Carol, turn him into a mad thing. Anyone would be a slave to your cooking. That Tom still hanging around, is he?'

Jenny said quickly, 'Yes, all the time,' and Mum looked hurt.

'Lucky for you he was hanging around in the market the other day, wasn't it, Jenny?' she said.

'He's only after yer dumplings, gel!' roared Dolly. 'And Billy, be careful of that Dolores. She's got all my boys round her little finger. That look will turn you to stone if you don't watch out!'

Billy was kneeling by Dolores, peering into her

face. He whispered, 'What's black and white and red all over? A penguin with sunburn,' and fell about laughing. Dolores stared at him for a moment and then turned her head to finish licking at her ice-cream with her tiny pink tongue.

'I think Dolores is a bit too young for jokes, love,' said Mum.

'And how's our Jenny,' asked Dolly. 'New school nice, is it?'

At the word school, Billy stopped staring at Dolores and ran out of the room.

'School is a sore point, I'm afraid, Dolly,' said Mum. 'Billy never wants to go and Jenny never mentions it.'

'Well it's so boring. And—Well, not all the children are friendly. I don't even know the names of everyone in my class yet.'

Mum sighed. 'Honestly, Dolly, Jenny used to love school. I don't know why this one is so different.'

'Tel's never liked school, never bothered with it much, have you, Tel?'

'No, Ma, I don't have the time, really,' said Tel, re-tying the pink ribbons on Dolores' skimpy curls. Jenny wondered how he could be so thin when Dolly was so huge. She didn't eat much at all.

'How is Walter, Dolly?'

Dolly patted her cottage loaf of auburn hair. 'Quiet as usual. Still with the gas board. And bored with the gas. He'll be there until he retires, man and mouse. But at least he's in work, thank God. So many aren't.'

Mum and Dolly went out on the balcony to look

at the view. Dolly looked like a ship's figurehead, gazing out over London.

'Gives me the palpitations, this height, Carol,' shuddered Dolly.

Tel laughed, 'Don't be daft, Ma. No problem. Look! This is how the pigeons go!'

'Don't you climb around there, boy, get down out of it!' screamed Dolly. 'Do you like hospital food?'

Then the noise from the flat above started. It was always bad on a Saturday afternoon. Over a frantic racing commentary from the television came a slower, flatter noise. It was a woman's voice, harsh, swearing, and spitting out words as if they were splinters of glass. 'Get out, go,' spat the woman. 'Leave me, you're killing me, I hate you.' A younger woman's voice raged back, cursing. A child began to cry.

'Leave it out, will yer!' roared Dolly. For a few moments the menacing voices stopped. But it began again, and the children were sent inside because of the swearing.

Billy tugged at Dolly's hem. 'Can I take Dolores to see my toy box?'

'Of course you can, darling.'

'Shall I make another cup of tea, Mum?' asked Jenny. She hated the angry voices from the flat upstairs. Sometimes she tried to find some music on the radio and turn it up loud, but the voices still pierced through like knives.

Jenny had once seen the woman with the vicious voice in the lift. She had sandy hair and a face turned away from other people. Her daughter didn't look very much older than Simone or Natina

83

and wore the same sort of trendy clothes and high heels. 'So much for women in charge of their own lives,' Mum had snapped. 'No babies at fifteen for you, madam!'

Jenny went to make a second pot of tea. Tel followed and hovered, eyeing the fridge hopefully.

At last he said, 'Well, then, Jen, who is he? Come on. Tell Uncle Tel.'

'Who is who?'

'Him. The old geezer with the funny green hat. Thought he was a Sikh, but wrong colour, he was grey. Him with the grotty dog.'

'Err-I'm not sure what you mean, Tel.' Jenny's hand pouring the boiling water from the kettle was shaking and she spilt some.

'He come round last weekend looking for you. He was hanging round your house like an old spook. Have you seen her? he goes. I goes who? He goes, the little girl, Jenny. Has she been back here again? Well, Jen, I didn't like the look of him one little bit. Maybe he's harmless, maybe not, but he's nutty as a fruit cake. It's a good job me Ma didn't see him, she'd have done her pieces, and set me old man on him. Or tried to. Well, young lady? Bet your ma doesn't know.'

Jenny panicked. 'He doesn't mean any harm, he's just a bit eccentric. PLEASE don't say anything, Tel!'

'I was cool, Jen, I was cool. I said you'd moved far away and I didn't know where. He just cackled at me like a hyena. As a fruit cake! And I said would he please get his grotty animal off of me ma's Grecian urn with the petunias. He goes,

"Sorry I displease you, young blood," and scarpered like Aladdin's genie. Done the swiftest runner I ever seen. Well, I didn't tell Ma and I won't tell Carol, just as long as you fill me in as to what a nice little girl I've known for years is doing friendly with a dirty old toe-rag like that!'

'Oh, Tel, don't be too hard on him.'

'You're a soft touch, that's your trouble, Jenny.' Tel opened the fridge door and peered slyly inside. 'You need saving from yourself. You may need some protection.' Tel pulled his shoulders back and set his face he hoped, to jut craggily like a real hard case. Clint Eastwood or the Special Branch, maybe. But the fridge door was still open and Tel's attention wandered to the trifle inside. Then he remembered his image and flexed his shoulders again. 'You may need a minder, Jen. What's the old nutter got on you?'

Jenny hadn't noticed the trifle and was impressed by Tel's hard man act, and concern.

She said, 'Thank you, Tel, for that offer. You see, the old man felt sorry for me and he gave me a present to cheer me up.'

'Never ever take off strangers! I'm surprised at you, my girl. Anyway, what was this so-called rubbish present?'

'A diamond.'

'A what?' Tel waggled his finger in his ear.

'A diamond.'

'You mean a bit of glass? Not a real one.'

'I think it was real.'

'Where is it? Give us a look.'

'That's the trouble, Tel. I've lost it somewhere. At school, I think. I've looked everywhere I can, without letting anyone know. Please don't tell, Tel. And I can't find the old man to tell him I've lost his jewel. I was looking after it for him. Where did he go?'

'Back under a stone, probably. Good God, gel, that's receiving stolen goods. You're too young for Holloway but someone would find something nasty for you.'

'Oh Tel, what shall I do?'

'Tell nobody, nobody at all. Honest, you shouldn't have taken it, Jen.'

'But it was the only nice thing that's happened . . .'

'Jenny, don't go searching out this old geezer, telling him you've lost his diamond. You don't really know him, or where he got it, or what he'd do to you.'

'I don't think he'd hurt me.'

'You'd go for afternoon tea with Jack the Ripper, you would. And how do you know it's a real diamond?' Tel walked with quick, jerky steps up and down the kitchen, fists clenched at the side of his leather jacket, ready for trouble. Once or twice he glanced at the trifle in the fridge, its whipped cream and pink hundreds and thousands almost casting a spell on him.

'I'm sure it was real, it was so beautiful.'

'You should have contacted me, I'd have made enquiries for you. I've got mates who know about things like that, it's their business to know. Mind you, they don't dress up in rings and bells with green turbans on their bonce, with a grotty dog from a freak show. Suppose you like waifs and strays, Jen. You're too soft, not hard like me.

Good God, gel, you ask for it! Let me know at once if he tries to contact you.'

'Yes, Tel. Actually he knows I live somewhere on this estate.'

'Oh Jen! Watch out, call me if you need me and don't go near the law whatever happens.'

'No, Tel.'

'And I'll keep my ears pinned right back in case anyone knows this geezer and his jewel. Now do as Unce Tel tells you.'

'Yes, Tel. Oh dear, how long has that been open?' cried Jenny, swinging the fridge door shut. Tel's dreams of sherry trifle melted around him. His face fell, then brightened as he saw a lone piece of fruit loaf reclining on a plate.

'I thought of going to Hatton Garden where all the diamond merchants are,' said Jenny. 'Oh— would you like that bit of cake, Tel?'

'Err . . . yes, all right. Needs eating up. What are you going there for?'

'Just to look, really. See the other diamonds and compare them. See if someone has found mine and is selling it there. It's so big, it would stand out. At least it's something to do, Tel.'

'Doubt if it's there, gel. But I suppose there's no harm. But don't go on your own, go with a friend.'

That's the trouble, thought Jenny, what friends have I now? Then she remembered Man Kit. He might go. Or Khadiza.

'If you see it, gel, do nothing. Call me. And keep that little mouth shut, whatever happens.'

'Yes, Tel. Thanks for all your help.'

'Any time, gel, any time.' Tel's cheeks were

pink. His eyes shone. He swept away a few way-ward crumbs from around his mouth. He strutted back into the sitting room and perched on the arm of a chair, smoothing back his hair.

'You look pleased with yerself, boy,' said Dolly, puzzled.

Tel smiled mysteriously and took out a clean handkerchief. He gently wiped chocolate from around Dolores' mouth.

Dolly, Tel and Dolores left at about five o'clock, and just before six Mum sent Jenny to the shop for some potatoes. On the way back, she found herself to her dismay getting into the lift with the angry woman from the flat upstairs and her little grandson. As usual, the woman ignored Jenny, but was engrossed in the little boy. She was trying to teach him to count sweets from her hand, chuckling softly. 'Tell your old Nan, then. 1 . . 2 . . 3 . . 4 . . 5 . . 6 . . 7 . . .'

The little boy said, '1 . . 2 . . 3, Nanny, 6 . . 4 . .' and looked up at her. They both gurgled with laughter. The voice which had razored the air a couple of hours ago was warm and low with affection.

Jenny was amazed, and thought about this for a long time.

She also thought about going to Hatton Garden, and asked Mum, who said, fine as long as she went with a friend and didn't get into trouble, or faint.

'Don't be silly, Mum,' said Jenny, 'As if I'd get into any trouble!'

Chapter Ten

'Is there a lovely garden at Hatton Garden, Jenny?' asked Khadiza, leaning over the bus seat in front.

'I don't think so,' said Jenny. 'I think it's lots of shops with diamonds and jewellery and rich people buying them.'

'I've never seen rich people,' cried Khadiza. 'Only on telly.'

'I know all about Hatton Garden,' said Man Kit, tucking the long white ribbon of their bus tickets behind his ear next to his pencil. 'I read about it in a book of London. A very long time ago, a man called Sir Christopher Hatton got a garden and a bit of a palace from a big Bishop. He paid one red rose, ten pounds and some hay for them. That's all! And the big queen, Elizabeth the First, liked Sir Hatton and gave him lots of money to spend on the garden and palace. And she came to visit him. Then one day she wanted all the money back, and lost her temper and shouted at him and Sir Hatton died of a broken heart! 'Cos she didn't like him and his garden no more.'

'Oh dear, oh dear,' cried Khadiza, twisting her long black hair round her hand. 'Poor man. But how can a heart break?'

'Too much sadness snapped it,' said Man Kit. 'And in Sir Hatton's garden were delicious strawberries and a cherry tree and saffron growing. Here is Saffron Hill on my map.' He stood up and reached in his pocket and brought out a neatly folded piece of paper which he spread out carefully. On it he had copied all the little streets of the area from the A–Z of London. He pointed out Saffron Hill and Bleeding Heart Yard.

'I know what saffron is,' said Jenny. 'My mum wanted to buy some but it cost two pounds for a few little squiggly bits. It's orange stuff out of the middle of special crocus flowers and it makes rice and cream cheese go yellow and taste nice. But I didn't know you could grow it in England. It must have been different in Elizabeth the First's time.'

'Sit down Khadiza! Do not bounce!' commanded Man Kit.

'I want to see, I want to see!' shouted Khadiza. 'I am so happy my father let me come out with you! And you are rude, Man Kit, you say my father is a Christmas father because he has long white beard.' She giggled.

'You are cheeky sometimes, Man Kit,' said Jenny. 'It's all right for you. They don't often let Khadiza go out on her own. Her big brother Rakib has to go too. And Mum doesn't let me out on my own now, either, just because I fainted in the market and met those coppers. But she says I'm safe with three of us.'

They stopped outside the first shop they came to. In the window there were some big crystals made into the shapes of swans and flowers with gold frames around them. There were huge rings with lumps of green onyx.

'Too big!' gasped Man Kit. 'Your fingers fall off. Look at the little camera over the door. Like an eye, watching us. It will take pictures in case we are robbers.'

Over the shop it said DIAMOND MER-CHANTS AND JEWELLERS.

'Come on, the search starts here,' said Jenny.

They hesitated on the creamy-pink marble door-step. Khadiza went in first. There was a thick pink carpet and big pots full of ferns. They looked perfect. 'Not real,' announced Man Kit, pulling a frond.

The walls were pale grey with panels picked out in gold paint. A chandelier like an upside-down fountain of little lights hung from a plaster circle decorated with gold flowers.

On the counter a slim white model hand trailed ropes of pink and flame-coloured coral beads. Fine golden chains hung from the branches of a gold tree. Soft music played, 'Diamonds are a girl's best friend'.

The jewellery in the display cases rested on circles of pink and grey velvet. Everything looked plush and expensive.

The children crept forward to look at the display cases. One was full of diamond earrings which winked like eyes. There were rings of every thick-ness of gold, some covered in patterns. Other rings had emeralds, sapphires or rubies in the middle of a diamond setting. Some had three or four or even five diamonds in a row. There were clusters in the shape of flowers and stars. The diamonds flashed and sparkled as if they were alive.

'Look,' whispered Khadiza. 'Look at that enormous diamond on its own in that ring. As big as yours, Jenny.'

'It says it costs five thousand pounds!' gasped Jenny. 'Suppose my diamond was worth that!'

Suddenly a voice squeaked crossly, 'And what do you want, might I ask?'

A small bald man with gold-rimmed glasses was scowling at them from behind the counter.

'We—we just wanted to look at the jewellery,' whispered Jenny.

'No children without an adult!' snapped the little man.

Jenny's face was hot and pink when she followed the other two out of the shop and found them hiding two doorways down. 'We weren't doing anything wrong,' she said.

'Smart shop, rude man,' said Khadiza.

'Hey, let's go in here,' shouted Man Kit, pressing his nose against the next window. There were pieces of sparkling rock in strange shapes, some mauve, some yellow, some pink. And there were polished stone eggs of crimson, sea green and indigo. Man Kit longed to hold them, roll them in his hand and feel their smoothness. GEMSTONES said the notice in the window. The children cautiously went inside. In the display cabinets were smiling Buddhas and Chinese horses carved from milky green jade. There were elephants of ivory and ships of rosy pink stone. There were jagged pieces of glittering quartz and rock crystal.

Khadiza was fascinated by a dragonfly carved from soft purple amethyst. It was as big as her hand.

In the centre of the shop were trays with hundreds and hundreds of tiny gemstones in every colour you could think of, from jet black through to pearl white. There were names the children had never heard of: peridot, cornelian, opal, moonstone, amber, agate, bloodstone, and zircon.

Jenny sensed a large shape hovering over her. 'Are you looking for something special, dear?' asked the big man softly. He looked like a barrel.

'I . . . er . . . I wondered where the diamonds were,' said Jenny.

'Diamonds? My dear, we sell semi-precious gemstones. Not diamonds. I know people who can get rough diamonds if you know what you want. But they wouldn't deal with someone of your age, I'm afraid.'

'Then which shop has diamonds we can look at, please?'

'None, dear. The only way you'll see diamonds in this street is in their settings, rings and brooches and earrings. Maybe a necklace or two. You can't buy them loose like gobstoppers.' The man chuckled. His glasses were so thick Jenny could not see his eyes properly.

'Who would I ask if I wanted to see some diamonds?'

'You'd need to find a diamond merchant, though why you're so interested, I don't know.'

How could she go to see a diamond merchant? Even if she had the nerve to enter one of those elegant offices, she couldn't begin to describe the diamond that the old man had given her. And it might really get her into deep water. Tel was right.

'What will you do if you see it, Jenny?' asked Khadiza, as they turned to leave the shop.

'I don't know. I sort of hoped we might spot it in a window, and then . . . I haven't really thought . . . I suppose I'd tell Tel and ask him to help . . . Thank you,' she called to the man with the thick glasses.

'Not at all,' he smiled.

Man Kit was fixated by a phoenix carved from orange stone the colour of a sunset, and it took Khadiza and Jenny a while to drag him away. He kept muttering, 'Two hundred and fifty pounds . . . my birthday maybe? Granny Kong . . . two hundred and fifty pounds . . .'

They wandered down the street, past many strange shops. One sold nothing but cigars. One specialized in pearls, milky white necklaces and bracelets lying on midnight blue velvet. Another shop had pretty brushes and mirrors and compacts of Wedgewood or rose-patterned china.

Man Kit read out the notice in one window which said, WE BUY SCRAP GOLD. 'How can gold be scrap, like old iron?' he asked. 'And what does that mean over there? KRUGERRANDS— THE ULTIMATE ASSET, BOUGHT AND SOLD HERE. That looks like a drawing of some coins next to it. I wonder if they buy old Hong Kong coins, I got lots.'

'I don't suppose so,' said Jenny. 'I think Hatton Garden is all a bit different.'

Man Kit said he would buy them all ice-creams before they went to catch the bus home. 'You are sad we don't see your diamond, Jenny? I will make you happy with ice-cream,' he said.

'If diamonds are worth so much money, perhaps I'm better off without mine,' said Jenny. She was very disappointed.

'You could sell it and be rich,' said Man Kit, his eyes gleaming. 'Buy computer and fast car.'

'I'd rather have the diamond. Mind you, it would be nice for Mum to have lots of money. She could have a dress. She always wears jeans.'

The man at the ice-cream stall handed them three cones with tall shells of pink and white whipped ice-cream. He passed Man Kit the change from the five pounds Granny Kong had given him. Man Kit peered closely at it. He looked up at the ice-cream man who stared back, tight-lipped. Then he peered back at the change again.

'Ice-cream costs too much here,' snapped Man Kit. 'Need a diamond to pay for it. I am not a tourist!' He stamped on ahead, biting savagely into his cornet. He had still not spoken by the time the bus reached their stop.

'Look at me, Jenny, Man Kit, look at me!' shouted Khadiza, swinging round the pole on the bus platform.

'Be careful, Khadiza, the bus hasn't stopped!' cried Jenny.

'Wheee! Watch me! Wheeee! Supergirl!' screamed Khadiza, her black hair and cherry silk scarf flying out round her head as she whizzed and whirled from the pole.

The bus stopped and somehow Khadiza missed her footing and fell on the kerb. Man Kit, just behind her, tripped over her and landed on all fours.

'Serves you right!' crowed the bus conductor. 'Wait until the bus stops, and don't muck about. Serves you right, young lady.' He jabbed the bell button angrily and the bus chugged away.

Khadiza, with tears standing in her eyes, poked out a bright red tongue at the conductor, who could do nothing but fume as the bus roared down the road.

Khadiza brushed grit and dirt off her hands, which were grazed and just beginning to bleed. Then she stared with horror at the torn knees of her pink trousers and the cut skin.

'Oh Khadiza, your scarf is ripped too,' cried Jenny. 'You must have stood on it and torn it when you fell.'

Khadiza shouted, 'Man Kit stood on it! My Uncle gave it me. My Father will be so, so angry.'

'Well, stupid wild girl . . .' said Man Kit.

'Shut up, you two,' said Jenny, 'Don't start bickering. Come back to my house, Khadiza, and get washed before you go home. And we could sew you up a bit.'

The tears had started again. 'It's not fair,' Khadiza moaned. 'My father will say I'm not to be trusted. They won't let me go out anymore.'

Chapter Eleven

'So people's bodies are under here, Jenny?' asked Man Kit, his eyebrows arched in surprise.

'Yes. Well, not really, 'cos they sort of crumble back into the earth after a bit, like old leaves. Lots of these graves have been here a hundred years or more. Look at the dates: 1840, 1867, 1842 . . . and the names are old. Hannah, Eliza, Samuel . . . I like the carvings on the gravestones. That one has a tree, and there's an anchor carved on the one over there. The man must have been a sailor.'

'Funny to put them in the earth,' mused Man Kit, nibbling on the end of a long stalk of grass. 'It is a lovely place. But better to burn up bodies when they are dead.'

'Shut up, Man Kit,' cried Khadiza, covering her ears. 'I do not want people to die.'

'Comes to us all, gel, each and every one,' announced Tel Jones. He pointed to a large gravestone by the side of the gravel path. 'Did you ever! It's a copper, hoping to go to heaven.' And he read out,

Sergeant Joseph Joyce, CID,
who lost his life while arresting a thief at

Charing Cross Road, 20th June 1892.
Although mortally wounded by two revolver shots he gallantly struggled with his prisoner until assistance arrived.

Tel pulled a face. 'Now he's gone to the Big Nick in the sky.'

Billy wasn't well that day, so Mum had had to stay at home with him and Tel had come to meet Jenny from school. Dolores was with him in the baby buggy, crowned with a large pink sunhat and shaded by a lacy parasol to protect her delicate skin.

For a change they had decided to take a short cut through the cemetery. Man Kit, Khadiza and Khadiza's brother, Rakib, had joined them. Rakib had accompanied Khadiza everywhere since her fall from the bus. Khadiza was furious, and would not look at him when he came to meet her from school.

The first time they'd met, Rakib and Tel had eyed each other warily and said not a word. Rakib had told Khadiza he did not trust any English boys, especially one with an earring in his ear. Tel had said he'd nothing against Pakis really, but didn't they all stink of garlic? Now Tel whistled and Rakib scowled, and Khadiza and Jenny couldn't stop giggling at them.

'Let's sit by those fairies,' said Khadiza.

'They're angels,' said Jenny.

It was a hot, sticky day, but in the cemetery it was green and shady. They sat down in a little clearing among the sycamore trees. Cow parsley grew all around, the milky flowers like lace. They smelled warm and sweet. Glossy-leaved ivy wandered over the ground and the graves.

Rakib stood proudly a little way apart, his arms folded. But he couldn't keep this up for long, and soon started to hunt for ripe blackberries.

'Phew, it ain't half hot,' gasped Tel, wiping his forehead with the back of his hand. 'Weatherman on telly said we'd have a bit of bother today, maybe a storm later on. Now on a hot day such as this, what does a man need? He needs chips. You lot sit tight and I'll slope off for chips and a coupla wallies. I'm starved. And Dolores is partial to a nice chip or three. Any orders, gents and gentesses?'

'Lots of salt and vinegar for me,' said Man Kit eagerly.

Khadiza wrinkled her nose. 'Ugh. No slimy chips for me.'

'I will have chips,' said Rakib. 'And one wally.'

'Same for me, too, please, Tel,' said Jenny.

'Right then. That's five chips and three wallies. You can have them on me. Even you, squire,' he said to Rakib.

'Oh no, Tel, you mean four chips,' corrected Khadiza.

'Five, gel. Dolores is well able to handle her own portion. But she can't do with a wally. You'll have to help me, Rakib. They'll be all right here. Stay there and don't move, you three.'

Tel, Dolores and Rakib went off towards the chip shop.

'Well, we didn't find your diamond at Hatton Garden, Jenny, but we had good time,' said Man Kit. 'Except for the bus.'

'You were so brave when you fell off the bus, Khadiza,' said Jenny. 'I think you should be a doctor or a nurse. You seem to like blood and horrible things like that. I hate blood. And beetles. And nappies and cat trays.'

Through a mouthful of blackberries Man Kit said, 'Lots of things to draw in this cemetery. Look at the hand on top of that grave. The finger is pointing to the sky. Why?'

'I suppose they hope the dead person will fly up to heaven,' said Jenny.

She lay back and looked at the blue sky through the green lattice made by the trees. It was so lush and green and quiet here. It was good to be with her two friends, she thought happily, and Tel would be returning soon with crisp, salty chips.

She listened to the bees buzzing in the white trumpets of the bindweed. Such a loud noise they made.

She also realized that there was another rustling noise from somewhere—a scratching, snuffling, rustling noise.

She looked behind her. There was a tall monument in the shape of a Greek column. The stone angel on the top had heavy carved curls and was playing a harp. The writing on the column was hidden by dark and twisting ivy.

Jenny stared hard but could see nothing. She began to feel chilly in spite of the sunshine. She leaned over and tapped first Man Kit and then Khadiza on their shoulders. She pointed. They looked over at the column.

Then, halfway up the column, a hand appeared

and clasped the corner. Not a carved, stone hand, but a moving, live one.

A head edged slowly out from behind the column, tilted to one side, the eyes looking straight at them. The children stared back.

A hopeful smile spread across the face. The green turban sparkled in the sun. Jenny was aware of faint but merrry music—trombones and cymbals from a brass band.

'Why did you have to creep up like that? You terrified us!' she shrieked. Ruby rushed through the undergrowth, looped tail wagging stiffly, and pushed her wet wiry chin into Jenny's hand.

'Funny dog!' cried Khadiza. 'Where is the other eye?'

'She lost it, dear. Lost her precious eye to a very nasty boy when she was a puppy,' said the old man. 'The boy was very sorry later.'

'Why? What happened to him?' asked Khadiza, but the old man just put his fingers to his lips and smiled mysteriously.

Man Kit was staring open-mouthed at the old man, who wore his glistening green turban, an old army shirt, the usual rings and scarves and a pair of outsize plaid trousers held up by a smart white silk cummerbund.

'Well, my dear. Things are looking up for you, I can tell. Your face shines. Real friends! I have been keeping my eyes open for you. And Ruby kept her one eye open too.'

'I've been looking for you, too. To . . . err . . . tell you something,' said Jenny.

'How very flattering. Flattering to be sought by you, Jenny.'

Poor old man, he'd come to see her and was pleased that she was happier, and all she had to tell him was that she had lost his diamond. Would he be angry? Would he be upset or dangerous? She hoped Tel and Rakib would soon be back.

'Hello, Chinese boy,' shouted the old man, squinting into Man Kit's face. Man Kit's mouth was still open in amazement as he clocked up the details of this strange man who grinned wickedly at him. Man Kit's nose wrinkled too.

'You're the one with the magic pencil, aren't you?' cackled the old man, and he tweaked the pencil out from behind Man Kit's ear, twiddled it round and tucked it back behind the other one. It slid out and fell among the cow parsley. Without a word, Man Kit searched for the pencil, picked it up and tucked it securely behind the right ear.

Khadiza was patting the snuffling Ruby on the top of her head, but squealed as a large drop of drool dripped onto her bare knee.

'I didn't know you were partial to graveyards, Jenny,' said the old man. 'I often spend a few nights here, but you're too young to spend much time with the dead. There's a mausoleum just over there which comes in handy for people like me. It's rather cold and damp, especially in the winter. They need central heating. But they like my music there. And my treasures are safe. Oh, time to go! My goodness, time to go . . . See you soon, see you soon.'

The children watched him melt away, puzzled.

'Is that the old man that gave you the diamond?' asked Khadiza.

'Yes. There couldn't be two of them.'

'Jenny, he is very, very funny. What will you tell him when he comes back?'

'I don't know,' said Jenny, worried. 'It's strange he didn't ask about the diamond.'

'Jenny, my father would not like that old man,' said Khadiza.

'Your father don't like anybody,' said Man Kit, breaking his silence.

'Well? You are frightened. I see the way you stare at him.'

'I am never frightened. But I never saw a man like that before. I don't like his hat. And he needs a bath. Let us go. I don't like it here now.'

'Why not?' said Jenny. 'It's a lovely afternoon. Just smell those wild flowers. And Tel is bringing chips. Why don't you like it, Man Kit?'

'Don't know,' muttered Man Kit, shrugging his shoulders. He picked a bindweed flower and gazed morosely down into its white trumpet.

Jenny said nothing.

Khadiza said, 'It is colder.'

It was chilly all of a sudden. A cloud must have hidden the sun. Jenny's legs felt cold in the shadow. The ivy which tumbled over the ground looked dark and bitter. It made her think of winter.

The silence was broken by the sound of footsteps along the path and the rattle of a baby buggy.

'Here comes my brother and Tel Jones,' said Khadiza.

Dolores, delicately nibbling on a limp chip, was being trundled down the gravel path towards them by Tel, whose mouth was snatching handfuls of chips like a mechanical digger. Rakib, cheeks bulging, strode along beside him.

103

'Here's yours, Man Kit my son, with mega vinegar and salt,' said Tel, handing Man Kit a hot greasy parcel.

'Thank you, Tel Jones,' said Man Kit, brightening as he unwrapped his chips and wally.

'Here's yours, Jen. And Khadiza, I bought you a fruit, seeing as we can't tempt you with chips and wallies.'

'Thank you, Tel,' smiled Khadiza, receiving the golden peach in cupped hands.

Rakib scowled.

'Glad to see you're still here, safe and sound, Jen,' said Tel, wiping carefully around Dolores' mouth with tissue. 'No old genies wooftering around!'

No one said anything.

If only I could find my diamond, thought Jenny, I haven't finished with it. I miss it.

'Right! Pushchairs roll!' commanded Tel. 'Eat up you lot, and home!'

Chapter Twelve

The next few days at school were worse than ever.
Jenny felt like a meringue that had gone soggy.
She could only face Man Kit and Khadiza and kept
out of everyone else's way. She worked away at
Mr Carr's reams of worksheets like a photocopy-
ing machine. At least they didn't involve much
thinking.

At home, she moped. She stood on the tiny
balcony and tried to remember the way the diamond had changed everything, but she couldn't
quite see it any more. She saw the concrete walls
of the blocks, spread with patches of damp. She
saw hardboard and corrugated iron sealing the
spaces where bright windows should have been.
Flurries of litter swirled like little whirlwinds
round the legs of figures hurrying between the
flats. They always disappeared. She could hear
voices shouting from the walkways below, but
rarely saw the bodies they belonged to. She longed
to stroll along a street and bump into Dolly, or
Mrs Ho and the children, and stand and talk
without feeling overlooked.

From the balcony Jenny could see distant trees,

but she knew that close to they were dusty and had sickly, patched bark.

The following Wednesday, Jenny sat on the playground bench waiting for Khadiza to return from home dinners. Jenny felt sick. School dinner had been greasy pink spam wearing a coat of even greasier yellow batter. Jenny wondered what the point was of killing the poor spam animal just to cook something so disgusting from it. The "vegetarian choice" was grated cheese, but it was not much of a choice because it was all there was every day.

'Jenny! Jenny!' she heard. Looking up, she saw Khadiza charging across the playground towards her, hair streaming out behind, and her face shining.

Khadiza flung herself down on the bench, gasping for breath.

'I know!' she panted.

'Eh?' asked Jenny.

'I *know*! I know who has it. I know who's got the diamond!'

'What? No! Who?'

'Yes! I talk to Hazara, you know, the new girl. Well, more new than others are.'

'But she's not at school today.'

'No. But I have seen her, On her balcony. She don't like school, she don't come. Norton pulls her hair.'

'But what did Hazara say, Khadiza? Come on, tell me!'

Simone and Natina, who were walking slowly past, turned their heads then pulled faces at each other and sniffed.

106

'Hazara tell me she have a better earring than me. I said good. She said only one earring, big and beautiful. She had to put an earring thing on to put it in her ear. But she said it is heavy and it makes her ear long like an elephant. So I begin to think. Hazara say she found this big jewel dropped in playground when she was late for school one afternoon.'

'Khadiza! It's my diamond, I know it is. Did you see it?'

'No, because her dad call her indoors. She didn't know it was your diamond, Jenny. You did not tell anyone at school that you'd lost it. Anyway, Hazara don't understand enough English yet.'

'Khadiza, will she come to school this afternoon?' cried Jenny.

'No, Jenny. She must help her dad sew. Maybe tomorrow she will come. Maybe tomorrow.'

* * *

That evening, Jenny sat in her room fretting and plotting for almost an hour. Then she had an idea.

'Mum . . . you know your friend Celia?'

'Yes.'

'Will you ask her to make another pair of earrings like those lovely bird ones she made for you? You know, the little bluebirds in the silver hoops?'

'Why?'

'Because I'd like to buy them off her.'

'Eh? You haven't got pierced ears so you couldn't wear them. And no, I am not paying for you to have your ears pierced. I don't care what other parents do, it's just ridiculous. You can sort it out yourself when you're sixteen.'

'All right, Mum, all right! They're not for me. You see, there's this girl at school called Hazara. She's new and doesn't speak much English yet and doesn't understand all Mr Carr's long division and stuff. And Norton pulls her hair. So—I thought she would like some earrings. She's got pierced ears.'

Jenny found herself examining her fork very closely as the blush spread over her face. She wasn't telling Mum the whole truth again. It didn't hurt anybody, she told herself.

'How very kind of you, Jenny,' said Mum.

Jenny felt like squirming. 'I can pay Celia for the materials,' she said.

'Oh, Jenny, I forgot!' said Mum suddenly. 'Celia isn't making jewellery like that at the moment. Evening classes have finished for the summer. But . . . in the meantime you can have the ones she made for me, I always forget to wear them. In the autumn I'll ask her to make me another pair when classes start again.'

'Mum! You're fantastic!'

'Aargh!' shrieked Mum, crushed by Jenny's hugs of thanks and delight.

Jenny ran to fetch the earrings from Mum's room. They were very pretty. The little enamel birds flew through their silver circles. But you couldn't see a different world in them.

Come on, tomorrow, Jenny pleaded to the sky through the window.

Chapter Thirteen

At last tomorrow came—another still and clammy morning. Everyone in the classroom was hot and cross.

When Mr Carr announced, 'Playtime,' Jenny was the first in the stampede out of the classroom.

She waited by the door to the playground as children hurried past. She became impatient. Then, long after everyone else, Hazara sauntered out, humming to herself.

Jenny pounced, pushing back Hazara's thick curtain of hair, first on one side and then the other, while Hazara shouted with surprise and annoyance.

'Where is it, Hazara?' cried Jenny. 'Why aren't you wearing it today?'

Hazara went on shouting. 'Oh, talk English Hazara!' said Jenny impatiently.

Khadiza's voice beside her said, 'She can't yet, Jenny, you know that. I will find out where diamond is.'

After a short conversation, which sounded very cross to Jenny, Khadiza said, 'She ain't got it, Jenny.'

'What? She must have! I brought these to give

her for it.' Jenny held up the little bluebird earrings, one between each thumb and forefinger. She dangled them like bait in front of Hazara.

'Look, Hazara, they match your lovely turquoise tunic and trousers.'

Hazara's eyes grew round as saucers. She stretched out her hand for the earrings.

'No. You don't get them till you give me the diamond, or tell me where it is.'

Khadiza translated what Jenny had said. Hazara hung her head.

'I no have,' she said.

'No have? Why not?'

'Him get.'

'What? Who? When?'

'Him get. Him Dean.'

'When?'

'Tomorrow.'

'She means yesterday, Jenny,' said Khadiza softly. They talked a little more, and then Khadiza explained it all to Jenny.

'Dean come to her flats yesterday after school when she play with her skipping rope,' said Khadiza. 'Dean took her skipping rope, then he see diamond on her ear, and say he will beat her with rope if she do not give it to him. Then he took diamond, throw back rope, and run away. Quickly.'

'Hazara, that diamond was my dearest thing,' wailed Jenny, fighting back the tears.

Hazara began to cry.

'Oh I'm sorry, it's not your fault. Dean was a bully to you. Look, Hazara, take the earrings anyway. They'll look lovely on you.'

Hazara stopped crying. She hung the little blue-birds so that they flew just beneath her ears. She spun round so that her long hair spread and the birds danced in their silver circles. 'Thanks, thanks!' she cried. Then she rushed off to look at herself in the mirror in the girls' lavatories.

Jenny and Khadiza looked at each other.

Khadiza said, 'I not frightened of that Dean,' and her eyes flashed.

'Neither am I,' said Jenny, which wasn't completely true.

They couldn't see Dean anywhere in the playground. He wasn't playing football, but Jenny knew that he was at school that day. She remembered him going round all the crates after milktime, emptying any leftover milk straight down his throat.

At last they found Dean round the side of the school, his fingers gripping the wire as he stared through into the Infants' playground. He was watching them play hopscotch.

Jenny took a deep breath. 'Dean! I want my jewel back! I know you took it from Hazara yesterday. It's mine. Give it back.'

'What jewel?' said Dean. 'I ain't got no jewel.'

'You lie, boy,' shouted Khadiza. 'Always you tell porky pies.'

'Shut it, Paki!' snapped Dean. 'It's the truth! I never had it for long. Anyway, that Hazara give it me. She said, "Would you like this earring, Dean?" Maybe she fancies me!' Dean placed a hand on his bony hip and posed for them.

Khadiza exploded. 'Fancy you! That is a big joke. You lie. Give it back, I have three big brothers at home!'

111

Dean's face turned pale. He stammered, 'I ain't got it. Honest. Look.' And he turned out his pockets in a panic. He had some change, his blue comb, fluff and a watch.

'See, the watch don't even work,' he cried, waving it in their faces.

'I don't see what that's got to do with it, Dean,' said Jenny. Why had she ever felt nervous of him? 'Just tell me what you've done with my diamond.'

'I was gonna find out whose it was and give it back.'

'Pull the other one,' announced Khadiza.

'It's the truth! I was having a look at it this morning in the corridor before class—funny jewel, innit—and that Spinner come up behind me all quiet and nicked it off of me. He goes, "No jewellery in school, Dean."' Dean mimicked Mr Spinner's deep, smooth voice with its home counties accent.

'You had better be telling the truth, Dean.'

'Honest! On my mother's life!'

The bell sounded for the end of playtime.

'If you lie, Dean, you will see my brothers,' warned Khadiza again as they headed into school.

Jenny believed Dean this time. Trust Mr Spinner to pick on him. Other children, such as Simone and Natina, came to school dripping jewellery. Nobody told them off. No wonder Dean saw everyone as his enemy.

Poor Dean. Jenny knew he would have sold the diamond given the chance. But it might have changed the way he saw everything for a day or two—just like it had for her.

Chapter Fourteen

Jenny hurried round to the entrance hall and knocked hard on the door marked HEAD-MASTER.

She waited.

Nothing happened.

She knocked again, even louder. There was silence.

Out from the room next door bustled Mrs Argent, the school secretary.

'He's out, dear.'

'When will he be back, please, Mrs Argent?'

Mrs Argent pulled a face. 'Your guess is as good as mine, dear. He says he's left me in charge. I can do without it, I can tell you. People knocking, phones ringing, parents fussing . . .'

Jenny went to look for Mr Spinner four times over the lunch break, again with no success.

But just before afternoon playtime she looked out of the classroom window and saw Mr Spinner's blue Volvo arriving. She rushed out of the room as soon as Mr Carr opened his mouth to dismiss them and flew downstairs.

Mr Spinner's door was already shut again and he did not answer her knock.

Just as Jenny was about to hammer on the door again, out of the room next door swept Mrs Argent, piled high with sheets of paper. She gave a light tap on the door with her fingertips and opened it without waiting for an answer.

'I should nip in now, if I were you, lovey,' hissed Mrs Argent out of the corner of her mouth. She plonked down the leaning pile of paper on Mr Spinner's desk, said, 'Sign now, Mr Spinner,' and bustled out again.

Jenny hesitated in the doorway and then made herself step forward.

Mr Spinner was sitting at his desk. His long hands straightened the pile of papers Mrs Argent had left.

'Right. What is it?' he asked without looking up.

'I've come to collect some lost property, sir.'

'What a time to come!'

'But you've been out nearly all day, sir. I've been about six times.'

'You should have come first thing. What is it?

'It's a jewel.'

Mr Spinner stopped signing and looked up.

'I beg your pardon?'

'It's a jewel. I lost it at school a couple of weeks ago.'

Mr Spinner stared at her. He had a thin face with white skin stretched tight across the bones. The skin was all blue–black around his chin where he shaved.

'Penny . . . Penny Postlethwaite, isn't it? New girl?'

'No, Mr Spinner. I'm Jenny. My name is Jennifer Fothergill. And I've been here since the middle of last term, so I'm not really new.'

'Right. Right. Jennifer, if you like. Well, there's no jewel here, Jennifer. And of course, you shouldn't have jewellery in school. I'm sure you know that.'

'But you *have* got my jewel, Mr Spinner.'

'I beg your pardon?'

'I lost my jewel in school. It was found in the playground by Hazara Begum. Then Dean took it off her. I know, Mr Spinner. They both told me about it. And now you've got it.'

Mr Spinner's face darkened. 'I have not got your jewel, child. It isn't here.'

'But you took it from Dean, this morning, first thing!'

'I did take the jewel from him, yes. He is not lying, for once, but I don't have it now.'

'You mean you've lost my jewel, Mr Spinner?'

Mr Spinner unfolded himself from behind his desk. He moved towards the window. He reminded Jenny of the spikey black shadow-puppet that Miss Williams had shown them at the other school. You moved its arms and legs by jerking sticks.

Suddenly Mr Spinner banged angrily on the window. A small first-year boy was standing near the window, not doing anything wrong as far as Jenny could see. He was in a dream. He jumped with fright at the banging noise and ran away, looking back fearfully over his shoulder at Mr Spinner.

Mr Spinner turned back to Jenny.

'I didn't lose it—the jewel was taken from this room, sometime this morning.'

'Stolen?'

'No one could have seen it—the door was closed.'

'But not locked? Where was the jewel?'

'Your jewel—as you call it—was on my desk. I was going to talk to the children about it in assembly tomorrow—I know Dean is a thief and I knew it wasn't his . . . I don't understand how it disappeared from my room. I don't know how anybody could have got in there and out again so quickly without being seen or Mrs Argent hearing them.'

'Mr Spinner, that jewel was worth a lot . . . to me, anyway,' she cried. 'How could you just let it get stolen?' She could do nothing now. She shouldn't have told Mr Spinner she had a diamond. She shouldn't tell anyone about it, especially someone she couldn't trust.

Mr Spinner frowned. He didn't say he was sorry the jewel had disappeared. He didn't care.

Jenny stamped out into the gloomy entrance hall. So she wasn't going to get the diamond back after all. That stupid, stupid Spinner. She wanted to cry, but she was angry too. She turned round and stuck her tongue out at the closed office door. That made her feel better.

* * *

Jenny marched through the playground door and came face to face with Simone and Natina. They drew back. Their noses quivered as if they were two centimeters above a smelly old cauliflower.

Suddenly Jenny saw how ridiculous they were. She laughed. Simone and Natina recoiled and looked at each other, horror-struck. They looked again at Jenny, then back at each other. They were appalled. But Jenny wasn't going to step out of their way. She wasn't frightened of them any more, was not even awed by Natina's expensive new leather-look purple jumpsuit, or Simone's hair-gel which smelt like flyspray.

They were just ordinary girls. And bullied by Jenny's grin, Simone at last let her lips twitch into what was almost a smile. It was troubled, but it was a smile.

For an instant, Natina's scared eyes looked into Jenny's. Then she coughed—a squeaky, nervous cough.

They sidled off.

The next person Jenny saw was Norton. He was lounging against the wall scowling out at the world from underneath his heavy brows.

'I like your new T-shirt, Norton,' shouted Jenny. Norton stared at her in disbelief. He glanced down at his new scarlet T-shirt, and then back to Jenny. Nobody normally said they liked him, or anything about him. He blushed and wandered off, puffing and huffing and scratching his head.

Man Kit said, his head on one side, 'You've got the diamond, Jenny? I know you are better.'

'No,' she said. 'No, I haven't found the diamond. But yes, I do feel better.'

And she went on feeling better, as if she had come out of a fog. At four o'clock she told Man Kit and Khadiza all about Mr Spinner as they ambled out of school. Mum was collecting Billy, so there was no rush.

'You don't mind too much now, innit?' said Khadiza. 'You don't mind too much about people. It's good.'

Man Kit said, 'Your face is shining, Jenny.' He cut the air with a smooth, flat hand.

'Jenny,' said Khadiza, 'you said your mum is taking Billy home today?'

'Yes.'

'But she is there. No Billy.'

Mum was running towards them, her face pale in spite of the heat. One of her sandals was flapping where the thong had broken.

'Thank God you're here!' she cried.

'Of course I'm here, Mum, why shouldn't I be?'

'Because Billy's gone.'

'Gone? Gone where?'

'I was a few minutes late picking him up from school, and the other children told me he'd been taken off.'

'Oh, Mum, Billy's not stupid. He's probably at home by now. He won't have gone off. It's his birthday on Saturday and—'

'Jenny, will you listen! He's not at home, I've run all the way there and back again. He's gone off with a stranger.' Mum fumbled to light a cigarette. 'Oh God, it's the wrong end!' she cried, snapping off the smouldering filter tip with shaking hands and lighting it again. She drew on it desperately. 'I'm going to get Mr Spinner to phone the police.'

Chapter Fifteen

Jenny began to understand. Horrified, she watched Mum's face crumple as the tears began to flow. She flung her arms around her.

'Don't, Mum, please! We'll search for him, we'll find him, won't we?'

'No you won't, you'll stay here with me, do you hear? I'll have to phone the police. Oh Billy, Billy, where are you? He could be anywhere, anywhere.'

Mum buried her face in her hands and sobbed. Her cigarette had dropped to the ground. The thin wisp of smoke curled listlessly upwards. The three children looked down at it.. They did not know what to do.

Then suddenly a little voice said, 'I'm not anywhere, Mum, I'm here.'

'Billy!' Mum ran forward and scooped him up, covering him with kisses. Jenny burst out laughing, partly with relief, and partly because Billy's face looked so cross as Mum kissed it again and again.

Then Mum plonked him down and shouted, 'Well? And what have you to say for yourself, my boy? Never ever *ever* do that again. Never go off with a stranger, I thought you knew that!'

'But he's not a stranger and I didn't go off. Only over the street and round the waste for a little walk. I was only a few minutes. You were late.'

'I'm sorry! I couldn't help being late,' Mum cried. 'Billy, I've been out of my mind! The other children said you'd been taken off by a man with floating scarves. They said that he waved at you from the gate and that you ran towards him.'

'They're daft. I know him.'

Jenny, Man Kit and Khadiza froze. Jenny asked, 'You *know* this old man, Billy?'

'Yes. I met him in the market once when you and Mum were spending too long on winter tights and it was boring. Then I saw him from our balcony. He was all glittering in the sun. I waved at him!'

Jenny, Man Kit and Khadiza looked at each other.

'And I've seen him near this school a couple of times,' said Billy. He looked up at Mum with big blue eyes and smiled at her.

Jenny said, 'Did you ever see him near Rendle Road? Or in the cemetery?'

'Don't encourage him, Jenny, for God's sake!' snapped Mum.

'No, I never saw him there,' said Billy.

How strange that we've both seen him, but in different places, thought Jenny. She stared at her little brother. Suddenly his face contorted—one eye closed.

She stared.

120

Billy's mouth leered down at one side and his eye opened and closed again. Jenny realized he was trying to give her a knowing wink. Why? It looked very funny. It was hard for her to keep a straight face.

'What are you pulling faces for?' snapped Mum.

'My nose is tickling.'

'Is it really! Your bottom will tickle too if I get any crosser and wallop you! Now I'd better go and let your teacher know I've found you after all. Wait there and don't budge. Watch him, you three.'

Mum hurried into school.

Immediately Billy said, 'You've got to go to him, Jenny. This evening. The old man. He needs help.'

'But where, Billy?'

'He's living in the underground car-park, near our flats.'

'What? I can't go down there, Mum says never go near it. How can he live down there?'

'That's just it. He can't. He's getting too old and he needs help and he's hungry.'

'I will come too, Jenny,' cried Khadiza. 'Oh no! Here comes Rakib.'

'You can't bring Rakib to see the old man, Khadiza. He'll tell on us.'

Khadiza stamped her foot and turned her back, refusing to speak to Rakib when he arrived.

'But I daren't go on my own down there,' whispered Jenny. 'Man Kit, call for me about half past six, all right?'

Man Kit began to protest.

'You must go, Man Kit. I told him all about

you and your drawing. He wants to meet you,' said Billy. 'Look out, Jenny, Mum's back.'

Man Kit frowned. He said nothing.

Mum gripped Billy's arm tightly as they set off for home. 'It's lucky for you it's your birthday tomorrow, Billy, or I'd keep you indoors all weekend. Promise me there'll be no more chatting to peculiar old blokes, or any other strangers for that matter.'

'He told me a lovely story,' said Billy, skipping along in spite of the pincer grip on his arm. 'It's called "The Story of Prince Billy."'

'Prince Billy liked drawing best of all. And he had a magic monkey. It had only one eye and that eye could only see half of the world. Prince Billy had horrible dreams. And he didn't like going to school. He was frightened of all the children who screamed and fought and he didn't like monsters.

'One morning he woke up from his horrible dreams. He was crying. Monkey was lying on the pillow. Monkey yawned.'

'How did the old man know you had a monkey, Billy?' asked Mum.

'I don't know. He just knew. Anyway, Monkey got dressed in his striped scarf and yellow jumper. He said, "Don't be frightened of those things in your dreams, Billy. I'm lucky. I'm a magic monkey. I have only one eye. I can only see half the world. So I look at the fine half, and the nasty bits just disappear."'

'Smart monkey,' said Mum grimly. 'I'm afraid some of us have to see the nasty bits too.'

'There's ways of looking so they're not so bad,' said Jenny.

'I don't agree,' said Mum. 'They're bad. That's that.'

'Magic monkey doesn't waste his time on them,' said Billy smugly. 'In the story, the magic monkey said, "Billy, get a big piece of paper and draw all the horrible things you're scared of."'

'And did he?'

'Yes! He got a great big piece of paper and drew big monsters and mucky classrooms and a cross teacher and a dad and people with balloons from their mouths and the balloons said, "SHOUT! ROAR! GRRR! GEDDOUT!"'

'Then the monkey said, "Have a good look at the piece of paper." And then guess what he said!'

'What did he say, Billy?'

'He said, "Scrumple it all up into a ball and jump on it, shouting, 'Treacle pudding with ice-cream and Smarties!'" That's a sort of spell, you see. Then Billy had won and all the horrors had lost. They disappeared for ever. The End.'

And Billy danced free and skipped ahead so that Mum had to run after him and grab him by the shoulder.

'I suppose that's quite a nice story,' said Mum grudgingly.

'It's a beautiful story,' said Jenny, and she could see the old man telling it. Then she remembered, with a jolt, that he needed her help.

When they got home, Mum said, 'I've got a lot of cooking to do for tomorrow afternoon, Billy, for your party. I can make the sandwiches in the morning, but I've got to finish the cakes and biscuits tonight. So sit down here on the kitchen floor where I can see you and play nicely with your lego—and don't move!'

Billy sat meekly on the floor building with his lego and glancing hopefully up at Mum every now and then, to see if she was still cross. She was.

It wasn't until Mum took Billy off to his bath that Jenny had her chance. She sneaked into the kitchen. There on the cooling trays were neat little armies of chocolate buns, butterfly cakes, ginger biscuits and oat cookies. Jenny took her shoulder bag, and some paper bags, and carefully collected one or two of each, spreading out the others so that Mum wouldn't notice. She also took some satsumas and a piece of cheese. As an afterthought she stuffed in a handful of tea-bags, and a tin of Pearl's cat food. 'Hope you like seafood platter, Ruby,' she said to herself.

'He's late, it's a quarter to seven. Come on Man Kit.'

Jenny fretted until ten past seven, when at last the doorbell rang. Mum got there first. She opened the door to reveal Man Kit, looking very serious, with his swimming bag over his shoulder.

'Hello, love,' said Mum. 'Are you coming in?'

'Going out,' mumbled Man Kit.

'Fine. You're not going swimming at this time of night, surely?' she said, looking at Jenny's bag.

'Oh. No. Just some books for Man Kit. Oh, and some fruit to eat.' Jenny blushed as she saw the satsumas glowing on the top of the bag. She zipped it up. 'We're not going swimming. Just playing out.'

'Good. Back by eight-thirty at the very latest. You can come back here too, if you like, Man Kit.

Madam here and her brother have given me some frights lately and I don't want her out late.'

Man Kit nodded dumbly.

'See you at my party tomorrow,' called Billy from around his bedroom door.'

'And Sui Han, too, I hope,' smiled Mum.

Man Kit nodded again.

As they went down in the lift, Jenny said excitedly, 'Have you brought food as well, then, Man Kit?'

Man Kit shook his head.

'What's in the swimming bag, then? Don't you want to meet the old man again? Meet him properly?'

Man Kit shook his head.

'What's the matter?'

Man Kit sighed. 'Jenny, I'm not coming with you. I do not like the old man. I am not sure of him. And the police might come. My family want nothing with police.'

'But you must come! I can't go on my own. Mum would go berserk if she knew.'

'You said he's all right, Jenny, so you can go meet him,' shouted Man Kit.

'I think it's all right, but you never know . . . it's silly to go on my own.'

'You said you trust him,' snapped Man Kit. 'Old tramp near us grabs tins out of litter bin and drinks any old stuff left inside. Ugh!'

'Man Kit, this old man isn't at all *like* that—he's not a tramp!'

'Oh? What is he?' said Man Kit triumphantly.

'Well . . . I suppose I am a bit scared of him. He's not really normal, I mean, not like a cosy old

Grandad or anything . . . and he'll ask me about the diamond and I'll have to tell him about losing it. Please come!'

'I'm not coming. I don't like his hat.'

'Khadiza would have come if she could,' shouted Jenny. 'Khadiza is much braver than you, Man Kit. She wouldn't have let me down.'

Man Kit looked hurt.

'I'm not getting into trouble with you. I would be punished bad. Mad old man! I have brought my drawing things. I will sit and draw outside the garage. I will listen and if there is trouble you call me and I help.'

'Thank you Man Kit.'

Man Kit smiled. 'Remember, scream loud and I will help you,' he said, and put his pencil behind his ear.

Jenny walked slowly down the concrete slope to the dark mouth of the underground car-park. She turned and waved to Man Kit standing at the top of the slope, his sketch pad in his hand.

Down she walked to the entrance. It was like walking down a big dim throat. Only a few of the lights were working inside. It took her eyes a while to get used to the gloom.

She hovered, not wanting to go any further. The car-park was larger than she had thought it would be. The roof was low. She couldn't see any cars. Patches of oil glistened on the concrete floor. The gloom thickened where the wide concrete pillars cast shadows.

Jenny dare not go right in. She glanced round nervously. Then she saw three cars in the far corner. They were metal carcases which had been broken up for spare parts. There were no engines left in them, no steering wheels, seats or tyres.

Jenny heard a noise. It was a sort of wheezing, rattling noise. It echoed softly around the corners of the car park and round the pillars. What was it?

There! The noise came again. She could see nothing, no one, only the three car skeletons resting on their axles.

Something wet and clammy touched her ankle.

Chapter Sixteen

Jenny was too frightened to scream or run. Something brushed against her leg.

She felt a fan of air around her ankle. In the half-light she saw a glowing circle moving just above the ground.

'What an honour, to be remembered with such gladness!' chuckled a voice.

Bewildered, Jenny stared around the gloomy car-park.

'I'm over here, dear, reclining in my chariot,' came the voice again from inside an old black Cortina with a gold sunburst painted on the side, right against the far wall.

'It is you, isn't it, Jenny?' came the voice, faltering.

'Yes,' she cried, and bent down to pat Ruby. The little dog's tail was wagging. She barked gruffly. They both ran over to the old man.

He sat up in the black car and adjusted his turban. For a second Jenny caught the scent of incense and old chips.

'These springs are very hard on the posterior,'

he wheezed. 'Thank you for coming so soon, Jenny owl.'

'What are you doing down here?'

'Doing? I'm living.'

'What? In that old car?'

'Why not? I had to move out of the mausoleum in the cemetery. It was so damp. Bad for the bones. And there were too many other beings drifting around.'

'Do you mean ghosts?' whispered Jenny.

'Oh, they were no trouble. But there were others . . . I must say, I don't like it down here very much. At least the mausoleum was decorative. This is so bare, and so mean. Anyway, I must move on, Jenny, on to the north country. I feel as if I can't breathe in London anymore. Though there were fogs when I was small.'

'You don't sound very well. That's a terrible cough.' said Jenny remembering her little vision of the old man walking on a hillside. He had looked happy, not ill like this.

'I was born in those hills, seventy-seven years ago. I remember them in my dreams. Soft wind, now near, now far, crying in the hills. There were fires to sit round at night, black nights sprinkled with silver stars.'

'Are you sure?'

'Yes. Then there was a fog. I don't remember any more just now.'

Jenny peered at the old man closely. His eyes, usually such a startling green, looked tired and filmy.

'Sit down, dear,' he said. There was an old car seat propped against the wall. The stuffing spilled out in a greasy yellow cloud. The old man dragged the seat towards Jenny and bowed elaborately, waving his arms in a circle for her to be seated.

At once, Ruby sprang onto Jenny's knee and curled up, winking at Jenny with her one eye.

The old man in his rainbow scarves and vast striped suit sat back in the car.

'Do you like my new suit?' said the old man. 'An Italian tailor made it. Rather Mafiosi, don't you know?' He swung his dirty feet in their leather sandals.

'It's very smart,' said Jenny. 'You don't look well at all, though. There's some cough medicine indoors. I'll bring it down tomorrow. I won't be able to come back here again tonight. Mum is so mad about Billy going off with you, she wouldn't let me out again.'

'Oh dear, oh dear me. How thoughtless of me. But Billy was so unhappy, and I wanted to help him with a story. It was his birthday present, to make him prince of his world.'

'Oh, you did help him, very much! And you helped me, with the diamond. Oh!' Jenny felt her face burn but the old man said nothing. 'Now try some of Mum's cooking. Look!' Jenny began to take out the cakes and biscuits.

'All these treasures from a plastic carrier bag!' cried the old man, smacking his lips. 'What delightful little delicacies!' Do you mind if I . . . ?'

'Go ahead!' cried Jenny. He popped a whole butterfly cake into his mouth.

'This is Mum's best cooking for Billy's birthday. She doesn't know I've taken them.'

'Lies for love are the only ones which may be

told,' said the old man, taking a chocolate bun and peering at the icing roughed up like little waves. 'The magpie bag is empty of food now, and most of my treasures are gone . . .' 'They're following me, you see . . .' His voice trailed away into silence.

Sure enough, the big black bag with the bird clasp seemed curiously empty and deflated, except for the bottom which was filled out with something squarish.

'Are those books?' asked Jenny, pointing.

'No. They are not,' he said simply. 'But what beautiful golden plums you've brought me.'

'They're satsumas,' said Jenny.

'They're satsumas. Of course. My eyes are weakening. Except my third eye.' He chuckled and pointed to an oval brooch with a milky green stone which was pinned to the front of his turban.

'What do you mean? I wish you'd explain a bit more sometimes—I don't understand!' wailed Jenny.

'Look, Ruby, the finest cat food in the world for you. Now where is my tin-opener for this feline treat?'

The little dog dipped her whiskery nose into the opened tin and guzzled noisily.

'Poor Ruby has been living on custard-creams and old take-away boxes for the last three days. Poor Ruby pyedog. But she'd never leave me, nor I her.' The old man stroked Ruby's rough, skinny back. His hands were long and graceful but the knuckles were swollen above the big rings.

'Can you get your rings off?' asked Jenny.

'No, not now. My hands are useless now.' He

shook them sadly. 'Hands and eyes . . . Did you come on your own, Jenny?' he said, his head on one side.

'No. Man Kit is waiting outside,' said Jenny. She blushed. She hoped the old man's feelings wouldn't be hurt.

'Ha ha!' he cackled. 'Chinese boy, eh? Come to make sure that Jenny's all right, eh? And quite right too!' He wagged a finger. 'There are some very funny people around. Why didn't he come down here with you?'

'He's worried he might get into trouble,' said Jenny.

'Man Kit sees what is there,' said the old man. 'But your eyes see below the surface, Jenny.'

'Oh, why don't we go outside and then Man Kit can have a good long look at your face and draw you?' cried Jenny.

'No. Not now. It's too late.'

Sadness settled over the old man's face. All the wrinkles and folds of skin seemed to fall downwards. He looked very old. His green eyes stared at something far away from them. Suddenly he broke into a fit of coughing.

'I'm coming back down here tomorrow with some medicine,' said Jenny firmly. 'And more food. And I'll get some dog food.'

'Thank you, Jenny owl. You're the saving of me. And do you know what I need more than anything?'

'What? Tell me and I'll get it for you.'

'Batteries. Batteries, dear. For my music.' He patted his silent stereo. 'My little Walkman won't even crawl. As my eyes fade, my ears grow greedy.'

'I'll get batteries. And there'll be sandwiches tomorrow. Mum's making some for the party. Salad and cheese and vegetable patés and things . . . there'll be no meat, I'm afraid.'

'Good. One death will be enough.'

'What do you mean?'

The old man just smiled.

'You never answer my questions!' she shouted.

'One day.' He picked up the magpie bag and turned away from her.

Then he said, 'Close those owl's eyes and hold out your hand.'

Jenny did as she was told and felt a small cold weight placed in her hand. She knew at once what it was.

'My diamond!' she shrieked so that her voice echoed around the car park. The diamond sparkled at her.

'See how it shines and cuts this unnatural light,' said the old man.

'But how did . . . where did . . . ?'

'Take care of the diamond for me, Jenny.'

'But I lost it before.'

'I know. And you did all you could to get it back, I'm sure. See how it shines for you. I don't need it. I can't see its worlds any more. My eyes have failed so quickly these past few months. And if they come, they will take the diamond too.'

'Who will come? Who will take it? Where is it from?'

The old man put his fingers to his lips. For a

moment his emerald eyes burned as fiercely as they had ever done. Jenny dare not ask any more.

'One day,' he said. 'For the moment, you and the diamond will take care of each other.'

Jenny said quietly, 'I'll be back tomorrow morning with more food and the cough stuff. And I'll bring a spare blanket to keep those car springs off you. Ruby, I will get you some genuine dog food, not Pearl's fishy rubbish.'

Ruby wagged her tail, and barked. Her one eye rolled.

'Give Billy my birthday wishes,' said the old man.

'I will.'

'Jenny . . .'

She turned to see him smiling in the half-light, his turban and silken scarves shimmering.

'Jenny, don't forget the batteries. For the music. For my journey.'

Jenny went early the next morning, before starting to help with the preparations for the party. She had brought batteries, more food and a blanket, fruit juice, tins of dog food and dog-biscuits. She had to leave them all by the entrance. She called and called but the car park was empty.

The old man and Ruby were gone.

Chapter Seventeen

'Call that a motor, Rak?' Tel walked round and round the rusty old orange car parked outside the door of Jenny's tower block, now and then giving it a kick with his highly-polished white shoes.

The bonnet was tied down with string. The bumper lurched down towards the road and one headlight was all glassless and crumpled as if the car had got a black-eye in a fight.

Tel sighed deeply. 'If your mate paid more than a pony for that jamjar, he was robbed!'

Rakib ignored Tel's comments. 'My mate lets me drive his motor,' he said proudly. 'I will drive us to the Chinese Restaurant. Get in the car, everybody, and sit.'

'Easier said than done when there's no handles,' snapped Tel. He carefully wriggled his hand and arm through one of the little side windows. 'Good job a man understands locks, Rak, ain't it?' He opened the car doors to let in the three children and got in the front.

'Right, Man Kit, my son. Name of frog and toad?'

'Pardon, Tel Jones?'

'He means the name of the road,' said Jenny. 'He's got the hump, ignore him.'

'Oh. The Lotus Pool is in Half Moon Street, off the High Street. Hurry. My father will have the food ready for us in the take-away boxes, and we collect Sui Han for the party.'

After three attempts at starting, the car suddenly jumped forward and lurched off along the road out of the estate. The three children in the back shrieked.

'Watch it, Rak!' shouted Tel. 'And get in yer lane, there's another car coming. You get them on roads sometimes!'

Everyone sat without speaking. They were nervous and flinched each time Rakib, crouched in the front seat squinting through the dirty windscreen, moved the wheel.

'There is the Lotus Pool! Stop, stop! Next to Pearl's Patio Garden Centre!' cried Man Kit. Rakib stopped the car with a squeal of brakes.

The Lotus Pool was cool, dark and full of people eating their lunch. The air was fragrant with food.

Man Kit led the way to the kitchen. Jenny saw his father smiling through the steam as he deftly stirred and flipped the food sizzling in the giant woks. A neat little tower of sealed foil dishes was stacked up ready for collection.

'Thank you, Mr Kong,' said Jenny. 'It's really kind of you to cook these for us. My mum says thank you, and she's coming in to try your stuffed mushrooms sometime soon.'

'Have a good party,' smiled Man Kit's dad, cracking four eggs together onto a pan of rice.

Man Kit's big sister Sui Han was sitting by the cash desk waiting to join them.

Billy had specially asked if Sui Han could come to his birthday party. He had seen her meeting Man Kit from school one day and decided she looked so wonderful she must be out of a fairy tale.

The car spluttered into life and chugged off.

'Real old banger!' smiled Sui Han. 'My friend Wei Lon works in City and drives white Lotus.'

Tel and Rakib said nothing. Rakib scowled.

As the car lurched round the next corner, a movement on the road ahead caught Jenny's eye.

'Ruby!' she cried.

The little dog scurried across the road ahead of them and jumped onto the pavement. Her eye bulged and her ears were flat against her bony head. As Jenny turned to look Ruby ran on down the road.

★ ★ ★

There was just enough room on the table for all Mr Kong's food among Mum's cooking. Mum tried to organize games for Billy and the three children he had asked from his class, but they kept wandering towards the table.

So games were abandoned for the time being, and everyone hovered, their mouths watering, while Dolly, teetering on high-heeled gold sandals, served platefuls of food.

Then Khadiza's father arrived. He smiled shyly and looked much gentler than the ogre Jenny had imagined him to be.

'Just in time! We're into some serious eating

here.' said Tel, sloshing a whole polystyrene cupful of Mr Kong's plum sauce over his home-made pizza and chips.

Khadiza took her father by the arm and introduced him to Jenny and her mum.

'I'm so pleased that Jenny has made friends at school,' smiled Mum. 'And Khadiza is so full of beans, isn't she?'

Khadiza's father looked puzzled. Then he smiled and patted Khadiza on the head. 'Naughty girl,' he said.

Suddenly Tel clapped his hand to his mouth and hurried over to them.

'I forgot,' he said and looked furtively over each shoulder.

'You look a bit shifty, Tel,' said Jenny. 'Have a butterfly cake.'

'Ta, gel,' said Tel and popped the cake into his mouth. Then he pulled a piece of newspaper from his inside pocket.

'Now cop a load of this,' he spluttered through a mouthful of butterfly cake. 'It was in yesterday's *Gazette*.'

The *Gazette* was the local paper which came out twice a week.

Jenny unfolded the newspaper cutting and the others crowded round. Jenny read it out.

> Police and others searching for a man known as Nicholas the Painter now believe he may be hiding in this area. He is wanted in connection with a series of robberies from both public and private art collections.
> According to our art critic, Nicholas

Hardraw, (or Nicholas the Painter, as he came to be known) painted miniatures similar to those painted in the time of Elizabeth the First and is considered to be one of the finest British artists of today. His tiny detailed paintings show animals, gardens and people in brilliant jewel-like colours. They have that mysterious quality of being from another time and place. Several examples of his work can be seen at the Tate Gallery and the Royal Academy. Nicholas Hardraw vanished without trace ten years ago and all his paintings were taken into various private and public collections. However, many of his paintings have recently disappeared and the police think it is possible that Nicholas Hardraw himself has had something to do with their theft.

Nicholas the Painter was always an outsider. He was well known for his anti-social behaviour and outrageous dress. He never appeared to have any close friends. It is thought that since his disappearance he has been living as a down-and-out in this area. Anyone who thinks they have seen him are asked to contact the police on 01 488 1123.

'Does it remind you of anybody, Jen?' asked Tel.

'It might be him,' said Jenny sadly.

'I don't think it is,' whispered Man Kit. 'No dog.'

'I hope it is not the old man of the diamond, or he will have a bad time,' said Khadiza.

'Oh dear,' said Jenny. 'He did say there was

somebody after him and he had something at the bottom of the magpie bag which just could have been pictures. But he's gone now, gone from the car park on his journey, so if it is him, he'll be safe from them.'

Tel said, 'Don't look so worried, gel. He's a survivor. And it may not even be him. No mention of any diamonds or jewels. Or even a turban.'

'I bet it is him!' shouted Mum, pushing in and snatching the newspaper from Jenny. 'That old bloke that Billy's so fond of? So you know him too! I thought as much, Jenny Fothergill!'

'Oh Mum, don't be so snotty—!'

'Snotty? When was I ever snotty? Really Jenny! To call him an outsider, or eccentric, is putting it mildly. Bonkers might be a better word.'

'Well he's gone now. To the north.'

'But where is the diamond? Does he know? Has it gone for ever?' asked Khadiza.

'What's all this rubbish about diamonds?' said Mum. 'Come on, Jenny. Don't keep things from me, love.'

Jenny sighed. Then she reached into her pocket and held out the diamond to Mum, who took it, wonderingly.

'I'm sorry, Mum. I couldn't tell you before. But I will now.'

And Jenny told the story of the diamond. Most of it, anyway. She left out parts such as her plan to sneak out in the middle of the night searching for it, and the fact that she'd gone into the underground car park on her own. Something told her Mum wouldn't approve.

Dolly Jones listened too, tut-tutting. Tel was

trying to look as though he was hearing the story for the first time, head on one side and eyes wide with innocence. Dolly elbowed him sharply in the ribs saying, 'I've got you rumbled, boy, little Goody Two-Shoes. You should have looked after her, Tel, really you should.'

'I did, Ma, as much as I could.'

'He did, Dolly, really,' said Jenny. She told them how happy the jewel had made her, how it had helped her to see other sides to people and things, and how she had made up stories and dreams around it.

'It stopped me looking at the ugly things all the time.'

'I don't think it was only the diamond that helped you, Jenny,' said Mum. 'I think you pulled yourself out of your unhappiness. Poor love, I didn't realize you were so bad. But I've kept something from you, too.' Mum took a deep breath, and announced, 'Tom and I think we'll get married. Billy will be pleased, I know, but I haven't been sure how you'd feel about it, Jen.'

Tom, with Billy perched on his shoulders, was hovering nervously just behind Mum.

'That's great!' cried Jenny. 'Now you'll stop smoking and make puddings for every meal.' She kissed Mum, and after a little pause, kissed Tom too.

'Jenny, I'll be bringing Dennis, too,' said Tom.

'Dennis? Who's Dennis?'

'My cat. I hope he'll get on with Pearl all right.'

'They can share the cockroaches,' grinned Jenny. Mum smiled.

'There may not be many more cockroaches. The

Council reckon they will have finished the Rendle Road conversion in two or three months. So we'll be able to move back. And get a dog.'

Billy bounced up and down on Tom's shoulders with joy, pulling his ears so that Tom yelled, 'Stop it!'

'Mum, that's fantastic! Will we still go to Talbot Road school for the time being?'

'Yes. Sorry love.'

'Oh, I'm all right there with Man Kit and Khadiza.'

'We will all go to new school in September,' said Man Kit. The three grinned at each other.

Mum was turning the diamond over and over in her hand.

'Where did the old man get this, Jenny? Did he ever tell you?'

'No. He never really told me anything like that.'

'I haven't seen many diamonds in my life, but I do know they're supposed to be very hard. You can use them to cut glass, and draw pictures on glass. Let's see.'

Mum turned to the window pane behind her and dragged the jewel down the glass. It made a sliding noise and made no mark at all.

Tel said, 'Gimme the diamond. There's a way of making sure once and for all.' He popped another butterfly cake in his mouth as if for fuel and asked, 'Got a hammer, Tom?'

Jenny shrieked, 'A hammer, Tel? What for?'

'Best test, Jen, or so a mate tells me. I hit the diamond hard as I can. If it smashes into hundreds of tiny bits then it ain't a real diamond.'

Khadiza screamed and pummelled Tel on the

chest. Man Kit snatched the diamond out of Tel's hand and gave it back to Jenny.

'You're not hammering my diamond, Tel! I don't care if it's real. I don't mind whether it's worth lots of money or nothing at all, it's precious to me.'

'Sorry, Jen, sorry. I was just trying to help,' said Tel, blushing. 'It looks to me, Jen, as if it could be a crystal, Victorian or sommat. I have a mate who'd know if you want me to find out. Could be an antique.'

'I think Jenny is quite happy with the jewel as it is,' said Mum.

Jenny looked round the room. Billy and his friends from school were playing with his birthday presents with the monkey propped up in a chair, watching. Everyone else was talking, eating or laughing. Tel was doing all three as well as feeding Dolores with a pancake roll.

Then he plonked Dolores onto Rakib, who almost dropped her, and hollered, 'Gents and gentesses! Silence for Mrs Dolly Jones.'

Dolly clambered up onto the settee in her strappy gold sandals and swayed on the cushions, large and glowing.

'Please do not fall off, madam,' cried Khadiza's father. 'Pizza is below!' He pointed to some plates of food on the floor.

'Worry not, Nazrul love,' beamed Dolly. She raised her glass high and, lurching on her treacherous heels, proposed a toast to Tom and Carol and wished Billy a Happy Birthday.

Suddenly everyone shrieked as Dolly caught her

gold heel in the cushions and toppled down onto the floor.

She lifted out a plate from somewhere underneath her. 'Anyone for pizza?' She giggled.

Jenny saw that everyone in the room looked happy, all these special people. 'Joy for Jenny,' she remembered the old man saying, and smiled to herself.

But then she saw again in her mind Ruby scurrying along the road. Alone.

Jenny held the diamond tight.